An Elegy for a Killer

The Wronged Women's Co-operative: Book 5

T E SCOTT

Copyright © 2023 T E Scott

All rights reserved.

ISBN: 9798853365445

Chapter 1: Mary

Many things come under the category of a parent's worst nightmare. A child going missing, a divorce, a call from the school on a working afternoon with the word 'chickenpox'. Mary Plunkett reckoned a four year old with candyfloss must be right up there.

"Are you sure you wouldn't like an ice-cream instead?" she asked, trying not to let her desperation show.

"No," said Lauren with all the certainty of a pre-schooler.

"I'll get it for her," Sergeant Walker said, opening his wallet and not for the first time that day.

Mary held her tongue. They had only recently 'come out' as boyfriend and girlfriend to the kids and Walker was trying to impress them. He had quickly worked out that the best way to do that was to ply them with treats. Eventually, the novelty would wear off, but for the moment she was happy to let him work his magic. Vikki had already given him a thumbs up, which for a ten year old was a glowing recommendation.

"It's huge!" Lauren said when the vendor handed over a pink spun sugar concoction that was bigger than her head.

"Hold it carefully," Mary said, trying not to look at the stickiness that was already settling all over her child's face and hands.

"It's all right this place, isn't it," Walker said with a grin.

Mary had to agree. It was the first week in July and the school holidays were already new enough that no one was wishing the kids were back at school, not even their parents. It was the summer Gala Day and people wandered around the centre of Invergryff in sunglasses and shorts, with bemused looks at the round warm thing up in the sky. Noses were turning pink and cardigans were coming off.

A bead of sweat trickled down Mary's back and she huffed out a breath. "Can we find a bench somewhere? I'm cooking in this heat."

"It's twenty-four degrees," Walker replied. He looked like something out of a men's health magazine, a tight black t-shirt over his chest, his always slightly tanned complexion making him look almost continental.

Mary felt like a sweaty slob next to him. "I know, but I don't cope well with summer. And I probably should have worn something lighter," she said, giving a regretful glance at her hoodie and jeans combo.

"Much as I love your Jack Nicholson hoodie, you could take it off," Walker said, steering them towards a vacant bench right in front of Invergryff Abbey.

"It's not Jack Nicholson, it's Wolf from Gladiators," Mary said, outraged.

"Of course it is. Why don't you take it off?"

She complied, unzipping her top as the kids chased each other about on the grass.

Walker looked at her, noticed her pink t-shirt, and then laughed. "Where do you find these things? Is that Super Mario?"

"Yes. Um, he's getting married in a civil partnership with Doctor Robotnik. It was on sale."

For a moment she thought he was going to say something mean. Matt had always thought she was ridiculous with her love for nerdy fandom. More than once he had told her to grow up, or get over it. Looking around at all the other mums in their ditsy print dresses and perfectly manicured nails, Mary wondered if he might have been right.

"I love it," Walker said, pulling her close so that he could kiss the top of her head. "How else would I have ever known that Mario would wear white?"

She grinned, then quickly checked that she still had four kids with her. Walker could be rather distracting, and Mary didn't want to lose any of them today. And they certainly didn't want a repeat of last week's 'I just wanted to stroke the penguin' incident at Edinburgh Zoo.

"Any chance of a seat?"

A large shadow fell across the bench. Liz Okoro was only a week away from her due date and she was at the point where her stomach loomed ahead of her like it was in a different time zone.

"Of course," Walker said, leaping to his feet. Liz eased herself down onto the bench and Mary pretended she hadn't noticed the creaking sound as she did so.

"Is Dave around?" Mary asked.

"He's helping Bernie with the coconut stand. Why she ever agreed to do it I don't know. She keeps telling the kids how rubbish their throws are. One kid in the year above Sean hit her right on the forehead with one, then bolted. She was going to chase him down before Dave stepped in."

Liz stretched out her swollen legs.

"How is the… you know," Walker said, gesturing at Liz's bump.

"Oh, fine. I mean, I can't tie my shoelaces, but the baby is doing well. Apparently it's measuring big for the dates."

"No?" Mary tried to look surprised, but couldn't hide her smile.

Liz swatted at her arm. "Shut up, I know I'm a whale."

"A very beautiful whale," Mary said loyally.

"A narwhal," Vikki, her ten year old, piped up. "Like an undersea unicorn."

"I'll take that," Liz said with a smile.

Mary was about to add something about orcas when she felt a wriggle from a small person next to her.

"It's stuck!" A small voice wailed. Mary looked down to see

that, sure enough, Lauren had managed to wedge the candyfloss through the bars of the bench.

"I'll get it," Mary said, jumping to her feet. "Just don't start pulling…"

As soon as she said it, she was too late. Lauren, chubby toddler legs planted on either side of her, yanked the candyfloss out of the bench and went flying backwards. On her way, she collected Mary and they both landed on the grass with a thump.

"Oof." Her daughter had landed right on Mary's chest, forcing the air out of her.

"Mum, it's in my hair!" Lauren wailed.

"I know darling," Mary said with a sigh, pulling a clump of sticky candyfloss from her face, "it's in mine too."

Lauren was up and on her feet in a few seconds. Mary tried to do the same but winced when she put weight on her left ankle.

"Oh bloody… blooming hellmouths and shi… shiver-me-timbers," Mary said, trying her utmost not to swear in front of the children.

"Are you okay," Walker said, crouching down behind her.

"It's my ankle," Mary explained, managing to get to her feet with his help.

He knelt and rotated the offending joint carefully. "It's just a sprain, I think. But we better see if you can walk on it. If not it's a trip to the doctor's."

"I'll watch the kids if you want to take her inside," Liz said from her reclined position on the bench. "There's probably a first aid kit knocking around the Abbey."

Wincing, Mary nodded. "Thanks. We'll just be five minutes. I'm sure it's not that bad."

Although each step saw a dagger of pain shoot up her leg from her ankle, it was quite nice when Walker led her inside the cool interior of the Abbey. Invergryff's finest building, it was all gothic arches, stained glass and guilty hush.

"Let's ask about that first aid kit," Walker said, scouting around the place with a fierce expression. Mary found it rather attractive how capable he was in a crisis.

"I think I'm okay," she said, leaning on a pew and wiggling her toes. "Honestly, I don't think it's that bad."

"All right," Walker said, deflating a little. "Let's just rest it for a minute, then we'll see how it is."

There were a few tourists walking around the Abbey, phones out to take pictures of the architecture. It was probably very significant if you knew anything about Christian buildings, but Mary didn't have a clue. It was hard not to be impressed however by the height of the place and the age of the worn stones beneath their feet.

"I've never been in here before," Walker said.

"I was here at Christmas time. They had a carol evening.

Bernie dragged us all along because the ticket money went towards the care home. I thought it would be dull, but it was actually kind of... awesome." Mary flapped her hands trying to explain what she had felt at the time. "It's like... with the candles, and the echoes of the voices, and the stained glass... you can understand why people believed in this stuff. Back before there was telly and pizza delivery."

"Some people still believe," Walker reminded her.

"Oh yeah, I forgot," Mary said. Her ankle was starting to ease up and she was starting to feel a little silly for having caused such a fuss.

"Do you want to try hobbling about a bit?"

With the aid of Walker's arm, Mary managed to walk slowly up the aisle of the church. They reached the altar at the front and turned to one another.

The imagery suddenly occurred to Mary and she started to giggle.

"What is it?"

"Oh, nothing," she said, sure that Walker would be freaked out if she mentioned that she had been picturing them walking down the aisle together in slightly different circumstances.

There was a clang behind them and they turned to see something metallic bounce under a pew.

"What was that?" Mary asked. She noticed there was scaffolding beside them which went up to the chapel ceiling.

There were dust sheets and plastic around it so she couldn't see if there was anyone working up there.

Walker ducked under a pew and came back brandishing a metal trowel.

"They should be careful. If someone had been underneath that..." He broke off his sentence as something moved above them.

It happened so quickly, and yet Mary found that the moment was so clear she would never forget it. A figure fell from above them and thumped onto the floor of the cathedral less than ten feet away. She didn't want to look at it, but one glance told her it was a man, and that he was dead.

"Oh no," she whispered. Walker was already sprinting the few steps to the body.

He touched the side of the man's neck. Mary was glad that she couldn't see the man's face and what had happened to it when he hit the ground. It was bad enough to see the red puddle escaping below him and the crooked placement of his limbs.

"He's dead," Walker said, giving her the news that wasn't really news at all.

Chapter 2: Walker

"Stay back," Walker called to a group of people who were hurrying over towards the man who fell. He knelt next to the body for a few more moments, then stood up. There was no point in attempting CPR. Along with the extensive head wound from the fall, there was a long contusion on the man's forehead. And what looked like defensive marks on his hands. His gaze travelled up the scaffolding, but if there was anyone there they were hiding from sight.

"My name is Sergeant Walker. I'm afraid this man is dead. I'm going to call the ambulance and my colleagues, but I'll need you to all stay around for questioning. Does anyone know who is in charge of the Abbey today?"

A man stepped forward. He was in his sixties or seventies, with a bald head and nervous hands that twisted together while he spoke.

"I'm the Church Manager. Um, my name is Henry Smail. I… well, I just take care of the Abbey building, do the tours and… Oh dear, how awful! It would be the Reverend in charge, normally, Reverend McDade, but he's not here today."

Walker had already taken out his phone and dialled the station, but he put his hand over the microphone to ask the Church Manager: "Do you know who this man is?"

"I don't… I'll have to check the sign-in book to find out his name. He's one of the stonemasons we have doing some repairs. They just... I mean, I'm not really involved in that side of things."

Walker glanced up at the scaffolding. It was so tall and shrouded in plastic sheets that he couldn't see the top of it. "Is there anyone else up there?"

As one, each person in the Abbey turned to look up at the scaffolding.

"I don't think so. He was the only one that signed in this morning."

Smail began to tremble all over. Mary walked over to him and put her hand on his elbow. Walker was glad she was here. She was good with people and the last thing he needed was for the old man to have a heart attack. "Maybe you could take everyone somewhere quieter," Walker said, catching her eye.

"All right," Mary replied. She began to collect all the witnesses together — there were at least a dozen of them — and led them away from the body to the small side chapel.

"Mr Smail, can you close the exits," Walker asked. "Until backup comes I don't want anyone else walking in and no one is to leave until I've taken all the statements."

He looked up once more at the scaffolding. There was something about this body that he didn't like. Not just the fact that it had appeared practically at his feet. There was a mark on the victim's forehead like it had been hit by something hard. Caused by the fall, perhaps, only the man had hit the ground on his back. There was just enough doubt in the back of the

Sergeant's mind that he wished he could check out the scaffolding to see if anyone else was lurking there. The idea of a killer climbing around the Abbey just out of sight, when Mary and a bunch of other civilians were around was... horrifying.

But Walker knew he couldn't indulge his curiosity. Unless he saw proof of an assailant, the most prudent thing to do was to secure the scene, make sure that no one touched the body and that the other people in the Abbey were safe.

Luckily, he had help on that side. Mary had found a small room behind a curtain from the chapel and had taken everyone in there, out of sight of the crime scene. He had managed to give her a quick thumbs up, but that was all.

It was a long five minutes standing next to the body before the lads from the station arrived. Within seconds the formerly quiet Abbey was full of people, from the high-vis jackets of the paramedics to the black caps of the police officers.

"You've secured the scene?" Walker's boss DI Macleod had asked when he arrived. The Highlander knew they didn't have any time for small talk.

"The one at ground level I have, sir," Walker explained, "but not up there."

He pointed at the top of the scaffolding. "I didn't want to go up there without backup. As far as I can tell, that's where he fell from, and if there was an assailant they are long gone. The Church Manager Mr Smail reckons that you can get out onto the roof from the scaffolding, so that'll be where he's gone.

The only other means of escape would be for him to climb back down the scaffolding."

"Which he didn't do?"

"No sir."

Macleod sighed. "This is a health and safety nightmare. Look, I don't want to send you up there, but I don't see that we have a choice. We need to make sure there's no one still there. I'm still hoping it's just an accident, but we can't assume that yet. Take Constable Williamson with you. He's just flown back from Tenerife so he should have a good head for heights. And I'll phone for the helicopter to come over and make a sweep of the roof area. They might find our suspect with their infra-red camera thingies."

Macleod looked unsure. The Highlander wasn't the biggest fan of technology, but Walker was secretly excited by the idea of a helicopter chase.

The DI called over a Constable who Walker thought must be Williamson due to his sunburnt nose.

"Seth here will go up the scaffolding behind you. I want you to stop when you reach each level and not move up until you both say it's clear. Got it?"

Walker nodded. He took a spare radio and baton from the Constable and stared up at the scaffolding. He wasn't normally bothered by heights, but the idea that there might be a violent suspect up above them didn't make it easy to put his boot on the first rung of the ladder. After a few minutes, however, the climb became more tedious than frightening, with both men stopping and checking for assailants every few seconds.

"You all right Constable?" Walker asked when they were nearing the ceiling.

"Aye. Wishing I hadn't had that fry-up this morning though. The way this thing is wobbling is making me heave."

"Just don't puke on the DI," Walker said helpfully. He dared a glance down and saw Macleod far below them, giving him a cheery wave. All right for some, Walker thought. One day he hoped to be senior enough to order some other poor sod to do the messy work.

"I think the next level's the top," Constable Williamson said.

Walker squeezed past the man and took a look. "All right, I'll go first. Now, I'm pretty sure that if there was an assailant up here, he's long gone, but we can't be sure of anything until we clear the crime scene. Be careful and don't take any risks."

Williamson looked a little queasy with sweat collecting in drops on his brow, but he pulled out his police baton and gave Walker a firm nod.

Walker took a deep breath, then pulled himself up the ladder to the top of the scaffolding. This level was hung with sheets of plastic to stop anything from falling down below. Not that it had helped the victim. In fact, at the end of the metal frame, Walker could see a section where a plastic sheet had been half-ripped off from the poles. It could be the point where the man had fallen. Or been pushed. Checking carefully all around him – not that there was anywhere to hide – Walker moved gingerly over to examine the rip in the scaffolding.

"All clear up there?" Williamson's voice asked from the ladder.

"Just let me check the roof access," Walker replied, turning around and retracing his steps. At the other end of the scaffolding was a stone ledge which seemed to continue around the roof of the chapel. Up above him, he could see the huge arched pieces of wood that had been holding up the ceiling for hundreds of years. Taking another breath, he did his best not to glance downwards as he stepped away from the scaffolding and onto the ledge. Sure enough, there was a small door that led to the outside.

Walker made sure he had his radio on and his baton out before trying the door. It was locked. He tried again, just to be sure, but it wouldn't budge. If someone had escaped onto the roof, they had locked the door behind them.

"All clear," he called down to Williamson and he made his way back to the scaffolding. Walker took out his phone and called Macleod.

"The door to the roof is locked. If there was anyone up here they've gone out that way and locked the door behind them."

"Got it. You lads better come back down then."

Easier said than done, Walker thought, but after a lot of swearing and leg cramps, he and Williamson made their way back down the scaffolding to the ground.

"I just need to nip to the loo," Williamson said, his cheeks a grey colour that contrasted with his sunburnt nose.

Bad day for the hangover to kick in, Walker thought as he watched the man scurry away. Macleod came over with his phone in his hand.

"This place is a blooming nightmare," he said. "I've just got off a call with the Superintendent. He says there's not much we can do about the crowd outside. Twenty-thousand people are at this Gala thing. We had the helicopter take a fly past."

"I didn't even hear it," Walker said, more than a little disappointed.

"That's my point. There are so many people outside they couldn't hope to identify a single suspect. I've had uniform take a look around the perimeter and there are plenty of places he could have climbed down from the roof. No one saw anything, but we're going to look into CCTV. You're sure it wasn't an accident? I'm billing a lot of man-hours here."

Walker shrugged. "I think there's the possibility of foul play. I don't like the wound on his head. And a trowel dropped down from the scaffolding just a few minutes before he did."

"You've got that, right?"

"Bagged it up and gave it to the crime scene guys."

"Good. We'll treat it as a possible violent crime for now. What about these witnesses?"

Walker coughed. "My uh… Mary is with them now, sir. She was next to me when the man fell."

He pretended not to hear Macleod let out a groan.

"You've told her this is a police matter, I take it?"

"She knows," Walker said, with more confidence than he felt. The truth was, Mary could be a little unpredictable when it came to respecting the authority of the police. He just had to hope she would realise what a serious situation they were in.

The witnesses were in a room that seemed to be used for storage, but someone had managed to find some chairs and cups of tea for the people there.

Mary hurried over as soon as she saw him. "I've started taking names for you," she said, holding up her phone. "I'm not sure that the tourists know much, but…"

"Thanks," Walker said, putting his hand on her arm to cut her off. Macleod was already frowning and he didn't want Mary to get his back up any further. "I'm sure the Detective Inspector will want to speak to everyone in turn."

"Right." Mary didn't look happy, but she put her phone away.

"How long will you be closing the Abbey for?" An elderly woman with a knitted cardigan and a printed scarf pinned around her neck with a Celtic brooch had scurried up to them.

"We won't keep you here much longer," DI Macleod answered. "Sergeant Walker here is going to take your statements, then you'll be able to go. As for when the Abbey will reopen, that depends on how long our investigations take."

"Well, I don't think that's good enough," the old woman said.

"The Reverend will be very unhappy."

"This is Mrs Button," Mary explained. "She works in the gift shop."

"Yes, it's myself and the girl. Young Jodie has only been here a week, see? What a terrible thing for her to witness."

Jodie gave them a tiny shrug that encompassed the fact that she was at least thirty and had not in fact witnessed anything. Mrs Button seemed to be around a hundred and seven, tiny and wrinkled but with the fidgety energy of a small child.

"We've never had trouble like this in the Abbey before," Mrs Button said.

"Have you worked here for long?" Walker asked.

"Thirty-seven years. And I've been part of the congregation since I was a child," she said proudly.

"Did you know the man that died?" Macleod prompted.

Mrs Button nodded. "Alexander Guthrie. He was from Birmingham originally, but he was all right despite that. He asked me to call him AJ, but I said Alexander would do nicely." Mrs Button sniffed. "We laughed about that."

Mary squeezed her arm. "I'm sorry about this," she said.

"Me too," the older woman said.

"Do you know if he had any family?" Macleod asked. He was on the radio giving news of the identity to the station.

"He was married, I think, but I never met her. He didn't say much about her. Just came in and got on with his job, not slacking off like you see most young lads doing these days."

"And he was a builder, was he?"

"A stonemason. It's skilled work, you see. Not just anyone can do it." Mrs Button pulled a hanky from her sleeve and blew her nose.

Walker turned to the younger woman. "Did you know him well?"

"Not really," Jodie said. "He came in to sign the visitor book every morning and he said hello. That was about it."

"And did you ever get the sense that he…" Mary continued, until Macleod coughed loudly.

Walker felt his cheeks redden. "Mary, perhaps I could get one of the Constables to take you home. I can pop round and get your statement later, if that's all right with Detective Inspector Macleod?"

"That's a very good idea," Macleod said. "I'm sure your children will be missing their mother. You have quite a few of them if I remember correctly."

A quick glance told Walker that Mary was not at all happy with this comment, but he managed to steer her out of the room before she replied to his boss.

"I'll get that lift sorted," Walker said, stepping away from Mary and going over to relay the instructions to a female Constable who was standing in the chapel. When he walked back over, Mary hadn't moved from the spot.

"Constable Flynn is going to drop you at home. Um... Thanks for all your help. With the witnesses and so on."

"That's all right. I'm glad I could be of help to the police," Mary said, her arms crossed.

Uh oh. "I'm sorry I've got to send you home, it's just... It's a murder scene, you know the rules."

"No, I get it," Mary said, trying to keep her tone light. "You're just doing your job, right?"

"Right. Er... I'll pop by later then."

"If you want," Mary said, then she followed Constable Flynn out of the chapel. Walker watched the door close behind her, then turned to see the pathologist and his assistants lift the dead man onto a stretcher. Off to the morgue, poor soul, Walker thought. Mind you, when he remembered the expression that Mary had worn when she'd left, he almost envied him.

Chapter 3: Bernie

The text came in from Mary Plunkett just before four and by five o'clock there was a full meeting of the Wronged Women's Co-operative in Bernie Paterson's living room.

"I can't believe you saw the guy fall," Bernie said as she placed bowls of lentil chips onto her dining table.

"I'm trying to forget about it," Mary said her mouth turning down at the corners.

"You better not," Bernie told her. "After all, we've got first dibs on the investigation seeing as you were right there when it happened."

"I think it might be Sergeant Walker that has the rights to this one," Liz said, adjusting the pillow behind her back. Bernie was a little worried that the pregnant woman might be too much for her dining room chairs, but they seemed to be holding out against the weight for now.

"But Mary was there too," Bernie added, "and she could have seen something vital, we just don't know it yet."

Mary rubbed her face. Her mascara was smudged under her eyes. "I don't think Walker wants me involved. He couldn't get me out of there quickly enough."

"You see? The police are scared of the competition."

"I don't know. It seemed like it was more than that. Like he was embarrassed by me or something." Mary's mouth turned down at the corners.

Bernie looked at her friend with her panda eyes, nerdy t-shirt and blonde hair that she had pulled into bunches which for some reason were tied up with those blue rubber bands that you got around junk mail.

"I can't imagine why –" Bernie began, but Liz kicked her under the table.

"I'm sure he was just focused on the case," Liz said. "Walker is a bona-fide Class A boyfriend."

"That's what I thought too," Mary muttered.

This was all straying from the important point at hand. "You said that Walker mentioned it might not have been an accident."

"Yes. There was a mark on his head that might not have been caused by the fall."

"Did you see it?"

"No. I didn't get that close. It was all just a bit… And seeing him lying there…" Mary trailed off for a second. "It was awful."

"Of course it was," Bernie said with a nod.

Mary looked surprised. "You're not going to tell me I'm being a soppy git?"

"No. Seeing someone die like that is unpleasant and it is

perfectly natural to be upset. I would judge you if you were anything less."

"Oh. Well, thanks."

There was a moment of silence broken only by Liz's chair creaking as she hefted herself into a more comfortable position.

"Anyway, I thought you didn't want us doing any more free cases," Mary said. "I don't see anyone paying us for this one."

"No, but think of the advertising," Bernie replied. "The Wronged Women's Co-operative solve Abbey fall drama!"

"I'm not sure we should be taking on another big case right now," Liz said. "I mean, I'm going to be on maternity leave at some point in the next few days, assuming this lazy baby ever decides to come out and meet us. And we've still got Lochwinnoch Drive to sort out."

Bernie mulled this over. "If only you weren't leaving us so shorthanded."

"I know, terribly selfish of me," Liz said.

"Could we ask Alice to step in and —"

"We could not," Bernie snapped, cutting Mary off.

"Come on Berns, we could do with the help," Liz said.

When did this business become a democracy, Bernie wondered. "You know how I feel about that girl," she reminded them.

"She's still sulking about Alice joining the Specials," Liz said.

Bernie frowned. "I do not sulk. I have valid concerns about my niece working for Police Scotland, a.k.a. our competition."

The others gave each other knowing looks which meant Bernie had to fight the urge to give both women a slap.

"Let's look at things logically," Bernie said, deciding to change the subject. "Is there any reason why we should take the Abbey case? Apart from advertising."

"Well, I was on the scene," Mary said. "And I did speak to the witnesses."

"And you were right there but you didn't see the killer?"

"They were fifty feet up!"

"Still," Bernie shook her head. If only she'd been there instead of Mary. She was sure she would have captured the murderer.

Liz stood up with an audible groan. "I'm dead on my feet. Can we make a decision and get out of here?"

"Okay, here's the official line," Bernie said, holding up her hand. "For now, we focus on Lochwinnoch Drive. But if there's any sign that the police are screwing up the Abbey fall investigation, we go in all guns blazing. Deal?"

"Ugh, I just can't read any more government documents about hedges," Liz said.

"Well, you're going to have to. We've never been in a position before where both sides of a legal dispute are paying us to trash the other, so it's our most efficient investigation yet."

"I still can't believe they agreed to that," Mary said.

Bernie laughed. "Honestly, when Mr Biggins found out that Mrs Mackenzie had engaged us on her behalf, he couldn't shuffle over to my place fast enough. He practically demanded that the WWC take on his case, and when I phoned up Mrs Mackenzie to ask if she minded the conflict of interest she told me to go ahead and prove the 'old sour-faced whinger' right."

"It's sad really," Mary said. "I mean, all this fuss over a fence."

Bernie shrugged. "A boundary issue. Wars have started with less. In fact, you could argue that wars are all about exactly that. Only instead of two countries sending armies at each other we've got Mrs Mackenzie and her garden hose."

Chapter 4: Liz

Since Liz had entered the third trimester, Dave had adopted a wary attitude whenever he entered the same room as her. With one week to go, he practically sidled into the living room.

"Can I get you anything?" he asked, like some sort of obsequious butler.

Liz resisted the usual response of 'You got me quite enough nine months ago'. "Some iced water would be great," she replied, forcing a smile. "Mary's kids always wear me out."

He sidled off again, his shoulders sagging with relief that he had made it out of the monster's lair with such a minor request.

The monster sighed, moved her pregnancy pillow to the other side and opened up her laptop even though it was after eight. Thank god for work. Bernie had threatened to make her take maternity leave weeks ago, helpfully telling Liz the statistics about the impact of stress on the expectant mother. Liz had been quick to put her friend right on that one. Staying at home with nothing to do was her idea of stress.

Her last pregnancy had been very different. She was still working at the insolvency firm, junior enough that she had taken as little time off as possible. She and Dave had just bought their house and they needed the money so badly she had gone back to work after six weeks off. She still felt bad about that one, even though Sean was too young to remember being dropped off at his grandmother's with a bag of nappies and bottles of expressed breastmilk.

This baby would have a different start. Bernie, for all her foibles, loved babies and there was no question that the new mini Okoro would be anywhere other than at work with his mother whenever she had to help out the WWC. In fact, between Bernie and Mary she'd be lucky to get any baby cuddles herself.

It was nearly nine at night when the doorbell rang. Liz groaned. There was only one person that would turn up unannounced at that time of night.

"It's your mother," Dave called up to her, even though Liz was already making her way down the stairs.

"No sign of that grandbaby of mine then?" Grace said, putting her head to one side and appraising her daughter. "You look tired."

"I'm carrying around a watermelon, that's why," Liz said, following her mother into the kitchen where the other woman got the tea things ready. Dave had already made his excuses and disappeared upstairs. Liz could hardly blame him. A heavily pregnant wife was bad enough without adding a mother-in-law into the mix.

"Have you been eating your meat?" Grace asked her.

"Yes, mama."

"Don't roll your eyes at me. You need to feed yourself up, keep strong before this little one arrives."

"It's not my first pregnancy," Liz reminded her.

"Ach, you're ten years older now."

Liz took the tea from her mother's hand. "Thanks for reminding me."

"At least Dave will help you," Grace said, nodding her head with satisfaction. "Your father never went near you when you were a baby. It was a different time."

"Not that different," Liz said.

"Well, it was in our culture. Men stayed out of the way and women looked after the babies. Of course, that only made us stronger. Have I told you how me and your Aunties from Birmingham put you in a sling and took you on a protest march after there was a National Front meeting?"

"Many times. You thumped a neo-Nazi with one of my baby bottles."

Grace leaned back against the counter and smiled.

"Happy days. Now, you need to tell me what days I'll have the baby, my nwa-nwa," Grace said, slipping into Igbo.

"Well, I'm not sure that I'll need you every week."

Her mother paused, cup halfway to her mouth. "What?"

"The thing is, mum, I'll be keeping the baby with me. I'll be working from home at the start anyway, and then Bernie is happy for me to take him with us on WWC business."

While she was talking, Liz could see her mother drawing her lips together tightly.

"It's not that I don't appreciate the help, of course," Liz added, aware that the atmosphere in the room was now several degrees chillier.

"I see."

Liz tried to think of a way out of the conversation, but nothing presented itself.

"You've got a friend that lives on Lochwinnoch Drive, don't you?" she said in a clumsy attempt to change the subject.

Her mother sniffed. "Abbi Musa. Yes, she stays in one of the cottage flats. You know, the ones that are four in a block."

"I don't suppose she would know the people that live in the big houses at the end of the street? Mrs Mackenzie and Mr Biggins?"

Grace shrugged. "I could ask her."

"Thank you, that would be a great help," Liz said overenthusiastically. She knew she was over-compensating for the awkwardness of the baby discussion. The thing was, Liz was actually looking forward to being around to see this little one grow up. She had missed Sean's first steps which had happened when she was at work, and the same went for countless nativities and football matches. This time round Liz wanted it to be different. She just had to find a way to explain all that to her mother.

"I better get back to your father," Grace said, pulling on her coat. "You'll call me as soon as anything happens."

"Of course. And you're still happy to take Sean when I'm in the hospital?"

"I'm always available to help my daughter," Grace said, and Liz pretended not to hear the edge in her voice.

When her mother had left, Grace pulled a non-alcoholic beer out of the fridge and tried to pretend that it was a proper drink.

"Everything okay?" Dave said, his head popping around the kitchen door like he didn't want to risk coming in fully.

"Mum's upset that she won't be doing as much babysitting this time around. Or she's upset that I didn't tell her about it. I don't know, it's hard to tell."

Dave ventured into the room and started to rub her shoulders. "Just stick to your guns and you'll be fine."

Liz fought back the urge to laugh. Her mother had always been on good behaviour with Dave, but if you had grown up with Grace Okoro as a mother you knew that she didn't give anything up without a fight.

Dave took a packet of crisps from the top cupboard.

"Not those ones," Liz piped up. "They're my favourites."

"What about the salted peanuts?"

"Lots of fat in those, you should probably avoid them if you don't want a dadbod by the time the new kid arrives."

Dave wagged a finger at her. "You sounded like Bernie there."

"Damn, so I did." Liz pulled him into a hug and rested her head on his chest. "Can you ever forgive me?"

"In about a week I will."

"When I'm a human being again and not a whale?"

Dave kissed the top of her head. "I couldn't possibly comment. Any news about the guy that fell in the Abbey?"

"No. Bernie was thinking we could take a look at the investigation, but I don't see how we'll have the time. Mary was kind of shook up about it."

Dave popped a handful of peanuts into his mouth. "You said the guy's name was Alexander Guthrie, right?"

"Yes. It hasn't been officially released yet, but that's what Mary was told in the Abbey."

"I think he might have been a client of mine."

Liz raised an eyebrow. "You sure?"

"I won't know until I check the files at work, but yeah, I think he was. If it's the same guy, he came in around a year ago after he'd had some minor surgery on his right eye. Removal of debris. We did a comprehensive check, but his vision wasn't compromised."

"That's interesting," Liz said, stealing the packet of nuts from her husband. "Would you have a check for me tomorrow morning?"

"Sure. But you're not taking the case, are you?"

"Definitely not," Liz replied. "Now help me up the stairs to bed."

"Let me just limber up first," Dave said, doing some mock stretches. "I wouldn't want to put my back out."

"Not funny."

Chapter 5: Mary

Mary woke up when the man fell. It was the noise of the body hitting the floor, that was what had stayed with her strongly enough to infect her dreams. She checked her phone. It was just after six and by the sound of it none of the kids were up yet. She pulled on her 'I Shot JR' dressing gown and went downstairs to make tea.

It was strange, when she thought about it. The Wronged Women's Co-operative had investigated plenty of murders. But to see someone die like that... Mary hadn't realised how it would feel.

She grabbed two biscuits out of the cupboard and sat down on the sofa. Walker had phoned last night, but he had only been able to talk for a couple of minutes. The investigation needed its Sergeant, of course, and she understood that. But was it too much to ask for a hug from your boyfriend when you witness a murder?

Mary blew across the surface of her tea. Was it a murder? Walker seemed to think there was something off about the man's fall, but she hadn't seen anything. Despite what Bernie might think, she was just a useless civilian bystander.

There was a clatter of feet on the stairs and a small creature launched its way across the living room.

"Wow, careful with the hot tea, Johnny," Mary said, placing her cup on the table as her son climbed into her arms.

"Had a bad dream," her boy whispered as he clung to her.

She dropped her head down and breathed in his hair. "Me too."

"Was yours scary?"

"Yes. But it was just a dream. It's your brain doing tricks in the night. When we wake up it's all done."

"Even monsters made from giant meatballs?"

"Giant meatballs?"

"Yeah."

She tried not to laugh, her mood lightening. It was hard to feel sorry for yourself with an eight year old burying his chin into your chest.

"Why are you all bony elbows and knees?" Mary asked, kissing the top of his head. "I need to fatten you up."

"Maybe pancakes?" Big eyes asked her.

She grinned and squished him in for another hug. "Maybe pancakes."

By seven o'clock all four children were sticky jam-faced and happy. Mary barely thought of the falling man at all until she got them ready and dropped them off at school.

It was one of the odd contradictions of being a mother that when the children were in the house shouting at each other and running around with stomping feet, you always wanted some peace. And then when they left the silence was almost painful.

Mary grabbed her laptop and switched it on. In preparation for her upcoming maternity leave, Liz had been briefing Mary on the legal side of the neighbour dispute in progress at Lochwinnoch Drive. Part of the case centred on how the area of a communal right of way had been decided, with lots of accompanying diagrams and maps.

It only took five minutes of staring at the figures before Mary shut the laptop with a groan. Before she'd had the kids and stopped work, Mary had worked as an environmental researcher, so it wasn't that she was stupid. There was just something about large numbers that made her feel like she was back in High School, trying to make sense of sums and formulae that made her head ache.

More tea: that was what was required. She got up off the sofa and clicked the kettle, just as the doorbell rang.

Walker looked just as handsome as ever, with his strong jaw and just the tiniest hint of stubble. Even the dark circles under his eyes just made him look moody and interesting, to Mary's eyes at least.

"Thank god the kettle's on," he said as he followed her into the kitchen.

"Long night?" Mary asked.

"And morning. I got home at three and then I was up again at six."

Mary handed him a steaming cup of tea. She still felt a trace of annoyance at being dismissed when they were in the Abbey, but his tired face brought out the need to play mother in her.

"I'll make you some eggs. Fried okay?"

"Perfect," Walker said. He leaned against the counter with his tea cupped in both hands. "Macleod has managed to get me a secondment to the Major Investigation Team again. He reckons it'll help my request for a move out of uniform."

"That's great," Mary said, breaking the eggs into the pan.

"Aren't you going to ask about the case?" Walker said, the tiniest teasing smile on his lips.

"I didn't think you were allowed to talk to civilians like me," she said before she could stop herself.

"I knew it! You're mad about me sending you home from the Abbey, aren't you?"

"I mean... not mad, mad. Not Captain Kirk shouting 'Khaaaan!' mad, but yeah, maybe a bit."

Walker curled a hand around her waist. "Would you say you were Arthur Dent when the world got blown up mad?"

"You listened to it!" Mary squealed.

"I did."

"And did you love it?"

"It was... very weird. But in a good way. I've already

downloaded the second series."

Mary grinned as she handed over his fried egg sandwich. How could she stay annoyed with a man that had listened to an old science fiction radio show just because she asked him to?

"I guess I'll have to forgive you then," she said as they sat down at the table.

"I did feel bad about sending you home. But I need to stay on Macleod's good side, and he isn't quite as... accommodating to the WWC as I am."

Mary tilted her head to one side. "I get it. Besides, with Liz being about to pop any day now, we don't have the time to take on another case."

"Is that what Bernie said?"

"Well, not in so many words. But even Bernie understands the practicalities."

Walker's mouth quirked up at one corner. "I can't pretend I'm not happy that I'll be able to investigate one case without Bernadette Paterson getting involved. And you're sure you don't want to be a part of it?"

"I suppose I do want to find out what happened. Just because we were so close to it all. But at the same time, I kind of want to forget all about it."

He gave her hand a squeeze. "I can tell you that at the moment we're still trying to work out exactly what happened. We think there was a struggle, and Guthrie was hit with the trowel.

Then he either fell or was pushed off the scaffolding."

Mary closed her eyes against the image of the falling man. "You have no idea who might have done it?"

"Not so far. There are a few fingerprints on the scaffolding and we'll have to see if there's any that shouldn't be up there. His wife has been informed, and I'm going to interview her today."

"Poor woman."

"Yeah." Walker's radio began to crackle. He stood up and walked into the hall. Mary looked at the egg congealing on the plate and tried not to mind.

A few minutes later he came back into the room.

"Sorry about that. Turns out there's been a possible breach of the peace and the Constables they sent out are asking for backup. Some neighbour dispute or something."

Mary was already getting to her feet. "It wouldn't be Lochwinnoch Drive, by any chance?"

Walker raised an eyebrow. "How did you know?"

"I'll explain on the way."

"Ah. You're coming too?"

She gave him a Look.

"Of course you are. Well, as long as you don't put the sirens on, I guess that's ok."

Ten minutes later they arrived at Lochwinnoch Drive with no sirens or lights on. Walker pulled up to where another police car was parked. Mary stepped out of the car and was eager to get a first impression of the place. She had spent much of the last few days looking at maps and diagrams of the street, so it was nice to finally see it in reality. The houses had been built in the nineteen eighties, and had been described on the original sales plan as 'executive bungalows'. Many had built dormer extensions since then, but the estate had managed to keep most of its green space and decent-sized gardens. At the end of the Drive there was a little cul de sac with only three houses off it. This, Mary knew, was where all the trouble was. She didn't even need to hear the shouting to tell her that.

Walker signalled that she should walk behind them as they walked up the drive of number twenty-five.

"They're in their late seventies," Mary said. "I reckon I'll be okay."

"Are you kidding?" Walker snapped, "That just means they're less likely to back down. And a big garden provides a handy amount of dangerous tools to hand, let alone Grandad's old shotgun hidden in a cupboard. Stay out of sight until I've checked it out."

Chastened, Mary kept a few steps behind him as Walker walked around the corner of the first house and into the garden.

The shouting stopped, but when Mary peeked around the bungalow she saw a scene of destruction. There were branches of trees flung all over the ground and a garden hose was dribbling onto the patio. Mary could see that the garden was usually tidy, with lots of containers of flowers and stone animals that looked at her with blank eyes. She shuddered. Mary had always found statues creepy, particularly after a certain Doctor Who episode. She edged away from a rabbit that was standing on its hind legs in a threatening fashion, just in case it was an alien in disguise.

Walker strode over to the fence where two people were glaring at each other. He took their names and explained that he had been called to a domestic disturbance.

"Domestic?" Mrs Mackenzie said. "There's nothing domestic about it. This man has trespassed on my property."

Mr Biggins was a skinny man with a bald head that he protected with a sun hat. He had those funny round glasses that were in style in about 1984. He was holding a garden rake in such a casual fashion that Mary was sure he had been threatening the woman with it before he caught sight of the police officer.

"What are you doing in this garden, Mr Biggins, if your property is next door?"

"I heard her snipping away at my bushes. She's trying to kill them off. I was only defending my garden."

"Huh!" If looks could kill, Mr Biggins would already be six feet under. Mrs Mackenzie might be pushing eighty, but she was powered by indignant rage. The woman was small and round and had wispy white hair that was trying to escape from a bun at the back of her head. Despite the warm weather, she was dressed in a tweed coat that made her look like she belonged on a country estate, not a bungalow in Invergryff.

"Is this true?"

"They block all my light. Can you see how my pansies are drooping?"

"Um..." Walker looked out of his depth. Mary remembered that his house had a concrete patio and not a single plant in the garden apart from some brambles.

"She went for my leylandii!" Mr Biggins said, pointing at the offending woman.

"I'm sure she was aiming somewhere else," Walker said quickly.

By this point, Mary had judged it was safe to stand next to him. "It's a type of hedge," she whispered.

"Right. Well, you can't go around destroying other people's property, Mrs Mackenzie."

"It's not his property. It's on my boundary."

"That is yet to be ascertained," Mary said, thinking back to the collection of documents that were waiting in her inbox.

"Do I know you?" Mrs Mackenzie said sharply.

"I work with Bernie Paterson," Mary explained. "We are close to getting legal clarity on the situation. If you just wait a few more days..."

"We never had any problems before this woman moved in," Mr Biggins said. "Old Esther Grant never minded about my shrubbery."

"Esther Grant had cataracts in both eyes you silly old fool," Mrs Mackenzie barked back. "She probably thought you had the hanging gardens of Babylon over there. Not that patch of weeds you call a garden."

"All right, that's enough," Walker snapped and both of the elderly neighbours looked surprised at his tone. "You realise that this is a waste of police resources? I could be out helping the public right now, not watching two people argue over a fence. Two people, who, might I add, ought to know better."

Mr Biggins dropped his eyes, showing a hint of shame, but Mrs Mackenzie merely crossed her arms and glared at Walker.

"Look, I'm going to be keeping an eye on you. On both of you, in fact. I understand that you have engaged the services of some investigators to deal with this issue," Walker said and Mary stood a little straighter as the WWC was mentioned. "And I suggest that you leave everything in their hands. If there is any escalation of what we've seen here today, someone is going to end up coming back to the station with me. And we do not serve tea and biscuits."

"We will be in touch," Mary squeaked as she turned and followed Walker who was already striding back to his car.

She tried not to notice that the sound of bickering had restarted before she had even climbed into the passenger seat.

Chapter 6: Walker

"Do you really not give people biscuits in the police station?" Mary asked as they put on their seatbelts.

Walker gave her a kiss on the cheek. "What, you think we give criminals treats when they come in?"

"Maybe a Rich Tea. That would be punishment enough."

He laughed, then glanced out the window to check that the neighbours had returned to their homes. They had, grumbling while they did it.

"I hope you lot can sort this one out. We've had a few neighbourhood feuds get nasty."

Mary grinned. "If they start any more of that nonsense I'll set Bernie on them. Besides, Liz reckons we've nearly got all the paperwork sorted. We just need to send it out to their respective solicitors then it should be fairly simple."

Walker didn't add anything, but he wasn't too sure. He had seen these boundary issues get pretty bad in the past. He decided he would keep a little eye on Lochwinnoch Drive, especially if Mary was going anywhere near it.

"Should I drop you at home?"

"Yes, please. Do you want to come in for another tea?"

"I'd love to, but I need to get back to the station."

He left Mary at her house, enjoying the chance to get a lingering kiss at the door without a gaggle of small children peeping out of the windows. When he got back to the station, he felt replenished both physically and mentally, despite the petty squabbles of Lochwinnoch Drive. His stomach was full and the nagging suspicion that he was in the bad books with his girlfriend had left. It was a pity that the criminal case wasn't going quite so well.

He hadn't mentioned to Mary that their unit had received one hell of a dressing down from the Superintendent the previous night. Apparently, the press had got word that a murder suspect had evaded the police despite there being an officer on the scene when the man was killed. The officer in question was desperately trying to keep his head down and out of trouble for the moment.

When Walker arrived at the police station he was given a note left by Macleod that said that the DI had gone to speak to the stonemason's wife. Annoyed that the man hadn't just texted him, Walker got back in his car and drove to the other side of Invergryff to the home of the late Alexander Guthrie. It was a small house on a quiet cul-de-sac of bungalows originally built in the 1970s. Guthrie's house had bags of cement and piles of timber outside that suggested he was doing some updating. It would never be finished now, Walker realised, with a pang of sympathy for his wife.

DI Macleod's car was already parked outside. Walker walked over to it and rapped his knuckles on the glass.

Macleod – who had been resting his eyes – opened the door

and climbed out with a groan. "I had a meeting with the Superintendent first thing this morning and I only got to bed at five. I'm staying in that dump of a hotel near the airport and I couldn't sleep for the noise from the planes. Still, could be worse. Could have just been told my husband was dead."

They both glanced up at the house.

"How did she take the news?" Walker asked.

"Shocked. Not faking it, as far as I can tell. We got a sedative for her and the neighbour came over to look after her. There's a family liaison officer in there too. The press will hear about things soon and that's when it'll get grim."

The name of the dead man was due to be released officially this morning. The press vans would arrive soon after. Walker generally tried to keep an open mind about people but it was hard to see the people who came to bother the bereaved as anything other than vultures.

"We're putting it out as an 'unexplained death' at the moment," Macleod explained as they walked up the drive towards the house. "Hopefully that'll keep the heat off while we check CCTV for suspects. If the post-mortem confirms it was unlawful killing, then we'll have to change our story."

For selfish reasons, Walker hoped that the post-mortem would confirm murder, purely because he had been the one to suggest it to the Inspector. If it came back as an unfortunate accident it would make him look a bit of a twit.

"We're going to do a quick interview with the wife now,"

Macleod continued, "assuming she's fit to answer questions."

Walker followed Macleod up the path to the house. The curtains were still drawn in the front room, which didn't seem particularly promising, but as they arrived the door was opened by Constable Flynn, the female officer who had dropped Mary home the previous day.

"Mrs Guthrie is in the kitchen. I don't think she slept much last night, but I've got her up and dressed and she's drinking a cup of tea."

"Is anyone with her?"

"No." Flynn's face was pale and there were dark circles under her eyes. "She says she doesn't want anyone. Her mum's heading up from Dumfries today to be with her, but she sent the neighbour home."

"Anything we should know?" Macleod asked. Part of the role of a liaison officer was to keep an eye on the family of the victim, and part of it was to see if any of them might turn into suspects.

"She seems genuinely upset at her husband's death," Flynn replied with a shrug. "They had only been married a couple of years, no kids. She works for the council in the housing department. I haven't asked about suspects or anything like that, I thought you would want to do that yourself."

Macleod nodded. "Thanks. Now I want Sergeant Walker here to take the lead with the questions, and Flynn if you could sit with Mrs Guthrie, keep an eye on her comfort. She had an alibi for yesterday, didn't she?"

"Yes sir," Flynn replied. "We've already checked it out. She was working in the office near the train station. Twenty people work with her and she never left the building."

Macleod stepped up to the front door and let himself in, the other two following behind.

"Mrs Guthrie?" He headed into the kitchen where the woman was sitting with an untouched cup of tea in front of her. She was a few years older than Mary, Walker thought, with hair cut into a smart bob and wearing expensive clothes. Her face had the grey colour that people got when they hadn't slept and her eyes were red.

Flynn was speaking softly to her, explaining who they were and why they needed to ask her some questions.

"Do you know what happened yet?" Mrs Guthrie asked.

Walker sat down next to her. "I'm afraid not. But I was at the scene and I can tell that we're doing our best to find out what happened to Alexander."

"You were there?"

"Yes. I saw him fall. It was very quick. He wouldn't have felt anything." Walker wasn't entirely sure that was true, but if there was an unwritten rule of speaking to the bereaved it was that you always told them their loved ones' deaths were quick and painless.

"At the moment we are keeping open the possibility that there might have been someone else involved in your husband's death."

Mrs Guthrie shook her head. "Constable Flynn told me that you were investigating suspicious circumstances. I don't know, it all seems so impossible. It's a dangerous job, working from height. You don't think he could just have fallen?"

"We're keeping an open mind," Walker explained. "But it would be useful if we could get some background on your husband's mood in the last couple of weeks."

She seemed to bristle at this. "He was fine. Same as ever."

"Are you sure?"

"Yes."

"And there were no issues in your marriage?"

The woman's eyes narrowed, but Walker knew he had to ask these sorts of questions. Not because he would get the truth, but because of how she might frame a lie.

"He was a good husband," Mrs Guthrie said. "A sort of old-fashioned guy, you know? He worked during the week, went to the pub at the weekend. A simple life."

"He didn't have any arguments with anyone? Any fallouts?"

For a moment, Walker thought she was going to reiterate the perfect husband routine, but Mrs Guthrie didn't look quite as sure about this one.

"Well... he could be difficult sometimes. Like I said, he was set in his ways. And there was the thing about money."

"Money?"

"We always seemed to be skint, even though we didn't spend that much. I think it was a mental thing. Alex hated spending money, even when he had it. He would squirrel it away. I always said to him you can't spend it when you're dead. Oh."

Flynn produced a box of tissues and it was a few minutes before Mrs Guthrie could continue.

"You were telling us about your husband's attitude to money," Macleod prompted.

"Yes. I suppose that was the only time that he fell out with people. If someone owed him money he would badger them until they paid it off. That sort of thing."

"Can you think of anyone in particular?"

"A couple of old customers. I'll look out the names. But I don't think they would... I mean, no one would kill someone over that, would they?"

Walker took note of the names, while Macleod carried on the questioning.

"What about the people he worked with at the Abbey?"

She took a sip of tea, then grimaced when she realised it was cold. "I don't really know any of them. He'd been there for six months or so. He was happy when he got the job as only the really good craftsmen get to do that sort of stuff. He thought it would be good for his reputation. There were three stonemasons, I think. One was old Sam Finlayson, he's been around for ages. Alex apprenticed with him back in the day. He'll be... god, he'll be devastated to hear he's dead."

"And the other stonemason?"

"Cammie something. Sorry, I don't know his surname. He'd come up from England for the job. I don't think Alex liked him much."

Walker's ears pricked up. "Do you know why?"

"He was working on the ornate stuff, the gargoyles, those sorts of things. So he got paid more, and that got Alex's back up."

Money again, Walker noted. Could the victim's obsession with money have had something to do with his death?

They asked a few more questions, but it was clear that Mrs Guthrie had had enough. Flynn stayed with her when the other two left the house.

On their way to the car, Macleod rubbed his stubbly cheeks. "A few names, but no suspects are leaping out to me at the moment. This case has got nightmare written all over it. If only you hadn't been in that blasted Abbey we could have all pretended the poor sod had fallen by accident."

There was a moment of silence.

"Have you had breakfast?" Walker asked.

"Breakfast? It feels like dinner time. I can't remember when I last ate."

Walker reached into his pocket and withdrew a cereal bar. He handed it over to the Inspector without a word.

Macleod looked at it like it was a grenade. "Why did you have this in your pocket?"

"Well, I've learned that you get a little… tetchy when you get hungry."

For a moment the Inspector looked like he was going to blow up, then he shrugged and unwrapped his snack.

"I'm not happy about this, Walker," he said as he brushed crumbs from his shirt. "You shouldn't be treating me like a puppy that you keep some dog biscuits for in your coat pocket."

"Yes sir," he replied, not wanting to push things too far. He knew that Macleod could take a joke, but it still didn't seem sensible to be too cheeky with his superior officer.

"And give me another one of those bars. We'll probably miss lunch."

Chapter 7: Bernie

A trickle of sweat made its way down Bernie Paterson's back. She planted her feet as firmly as she could on the floor and leaned backwards with all her strength. It wouldn't budge.

She swore. Then she took a deep breath. Then she swore again.

"Why do the instructions make it look so easy?" she moaned, flinging aside the Allen key. She flopped down on the floor and glared at the offending piece of furniture.

The Wronged Women's Co-operative were in desperate need of a new filing cabinet. Bernie, as founder, partner and Chief of DIY had taken it upon herself to build one bought from a certain flat-pack furniture store. Two hours later and all she had done was break one of her nails.

The doorbell rang. Glad of the distraction, Bernie chucked the instructions to one side and went to answer it.

"What are you doing here?"

Her niece, Alice, pouted her lips. "You asked me to come, right?"

A sneaking suspicion poked at Bernie's mind. "Let me guess. You got a message from me?"

"Yes. Last night."

Bernie's eyes narrowed. "Liz was here last night."

"I see," Alice said. "You didn't message me. Liz did, pretending to be you."

"Looks like it." Bernie tapped her foot on the step. "Seeing as you're here though, I could use a hand with this filing cabinet."

Her niece frowned. "I didn't come for DIY."

Bernie turned and walked back into the living room, leaving the door open in a way that suggested to the girl she could make her own decision. When Alice came in next to her and picked up the instructions, Bernie even managed to resist a smug smile.

"You've got that piece on upside down," Alice said, pointing to one of the sides.

"I know. I just can't get it back off again." Feeling a little more cheerful, Bernie handed over the Allen key like it was a sacred artefact. "You sort it out and I'll make the tea."

Five minutes later Alice had managed to remove the offending piece of chipboard and they had both settled down to drink their tea.

"So how's it going?"

Alice cracked a smile. "You mean, how is it going in the Specials?"

Bernie shrugged. She wasn't going to pretend to be happy that her niece was working for the opposition.

"It's fine. I mean, I've never had so many people puke on me in my life, but apart from that I enjoy it. And although we don't get paid a wage, the bonuses and expenses can be good."

"The pay was better with us," Bernie grumbled.

"Aye, but after you took on Mary you didn't need me anymore, did you?"

Bernie caught her breath. "I wouldn't say that was true."

"Oh come on, Auntie. I know you took her on as a secretary, but she's one of the gang now isn't she."

"I suppose she is."

The rain had started up again. Even though it was summer, the Invergryff weather liked to make itself felt. They listened to the hammering it made as it hit the roof of the conservatory.

"At least the police force is begging for people. I'm never short of shifts."

"I hope you're not feeling sorry for yourself," Bernie warned her niece. "I never could stand any of that. Look, maybe we didn't have that much work for you when Mary came along, but that's all about to change. Liz is having her baby and we're going to be short-handed. There's work available for you if you want it."

"I won't do anything that risks my position with the Specials," Alice said. "But if you need some surveillance work, taking pictures, that sort of thing… well, I suppose I could find the time."

And that was as close to a truce as the two women were willing to come.

"Fine," Bernie replied. "Let's get on with this cabinet."

Alice stifled a yawn as she took another look at the instructions.

"Tired?"

"I was up late working in the town centre."

Bernie gave her a sharp look. "You wouldn't have been anywhere near the Abbey by any chance?"

"You heard about the man that fell?"

"Of course. Walker reckons that it wasn't an accident."

There was a clunk as Alice put down the bag of screws. "Oh no, Auntie, I know that look. You're not getting involved in this one."

Bernie held up her hands. "I'm just interested, that's all. You know that Mary witnessed the crime, don't you?"

Alice groaned. "That's just great. Did Liz push him off the scaffolding as well?"

"Are you kidding? The Incredible Bulk can't get above ground level."

"That's mean," Alice said, although Bernie noted that she was trying not to laugh.

"I suppose I can let the police have a go at it," Bernie conceded. "And if they mess it all up, the WWC is always around to pick up the pieces."

For a few minutes, neither of them spoke as they worked on the excruciatingly complicated drawer mechanism. When they finally got it working, Alice said: "I did think of you when I heard who the wife was."

"Mrs Guthrie? Do you know her?"

Alice shook her head. "No, but you do. Mrs Bella Guthrie, but her maiden name was Passer."

"Bella Passer? You don't mean... not Annabel Passer?"

"That's right. Weren't you at school with her? I remember mum saying you didn't get along."

"Not get along?" Bernie felt the heat rising in her cheeks. "That woman was nothing more or less than a bully. She made my life hell, just because I was a fat girl. Oh, and clever, she didn't like that either. Wow. I thought she had died or something. Or maybe that was just wishful thinking."

"Well, just because you didn't get on with her, doesn't mean she had anything to do with her husband's death."

"Are you kidding me? It puts her right at the top of the suspect list. Nasty little Annabel Passer with her knack for ruining other people's lives. That settles it. It would be morally wrong for me to stay out of this case. I need to make sure that woman gets what's coming to her."

There was a groan from the other end of the filing cabinet where Alice had put her hands over her eyes.

"Please don't do this, Auntie."

Bernie leaned forward and grabbed her niece's hand. "When your mum was sixteen she was asked to the pictures by the most popular boy in school. His name was Ryan and he'd been born in New York, he had spiked-up hair, Nike Air Maxes and he was the coolest kid we had ever seen. He passed her a note asking her to meet him before the movie. Your mum spent all day Saturday getting ready, doing her make-up, then walked round to the pictures because our dad needed the car and couldn't give her a lift. Two miles it was. And when she got there do you know what happened?"

Alice wasn't dumb. "Something bad?"

"He never turned up. It had all been a fake. A prank, they would call it nowadays. Of course, this was before mobile phones, so there was no way to check. Your mum waited over an hour at that cinema in the pouring rain. Just so that Annabel Passer and her pals could have a good laugh on a Saturday night. Your mum, bless her, laughed it off when she went back to school on Monday, but everyone was whispering about her behind her back."

"All right, that is pretty mean but –"

"Just a shame for Annabel that someone didn't like what she did to my sister. The next day someone put up a load of photos of her bedroom all over the school, complete with her beanie baby collection. She had over a hundred of the creepy things on her bed. Bet it took her a while to get a date after that."

Alice's eyes were on the ceiling. "A man is dead, Auntie. Please don't make this about some high school grudge."

Bernie bent low over the drawer front so that Alice couldn't see her face. Annabel Passer! A name from the past and one that she would never forget. How many days had Bernie spent hiding in the girls' toilets, hoping that her tormentor wouldn't find her? The Bernie Paterson of today was a million miles away from the chubby girl that was scared of her own shadow. Bernie had had to exorcise that girl, along with six stone in weight, to become the confident, kick-ass person that she was now. But somewhere inside her, that girl longed for vengeance. Putting Annabel Passer into prison for the rest of her life would be a sweet way to get it.

"What are you laughing about, Auntie," Alice asked her.

"Just thinking about how the instructions said it was an 'easy build'," Bernie lied. "Now let's get this sorted by dinner. This doesn't count as overtime, you know."

"Yes, Bernie."

Chapter 8: Liz

We're taking the Abbey case.

The message had come in from Bernie that evening. Liz took one look at it, then threw down her phone and kept packing her hospital bag. A murder case. Just what they didn't need. She rolled up her favourite pair of pyjamas and added them to the bag. Bernie Paterson was a law unto herself. Well, at least it wouldn't be Liz's problem. If the baby didn't arrive naturally by tomorrow night, she was booked in for an induction, and a probable elective C-section on Wednesday.

It couldn't come soon enough. Liz had always taken pride in how she looked. She liked getting her nails done and she had many more weaves than her husband was aware of. But she was now in the stage of pregnancy where even the thought of a hairpiece just made her sweat. She had wrapped a scarf around her head and pulled on one of Dave's old t-shirts and that was about as glamorous as it got.

She flung herself on the bed and checked through the Lochwinnoch documents one last time. It looked like they had finally put together the case file for both parties involved. The problem was, Liz reckoned that neither of them was going to like the outcome. Still, she thought happily, that was another problem that Bernie would have to solve without her.

Liz put some jazz music on through her phone speaker and pulled her legs up onto the bed. She rubbed her bump, wondering if it was true that they really could hear what was going on in there. Dave was convinced it was true and had been playing Bowie hits at her for weeks. Part of her hoped that the smooth jazz might stop her baby from kicking her in the ribs for a bit, but it didn't seem to be working.

The doorbell rang. Liz checked the time. Just after ten. It was probably a parcel delivery, Dave buying something for the baby online. Well, they could leave it at the door. She wasn't going to do the stairs again.

It rang another time. She shut her eyes and turned up the jazz.

There was a pause, then the sound of someone unlatching the front door. What the hell? Liz pulled herself to her feet and tiptoed to the top of the stairs.

A shadowy figure was below and Liz could just make out a sweatband around their forehead.

"Bloody hell Bernie, I was just about to go to bed."

Bernie looked up at her. "I was out for a run so I thought I would pop in. You didn't reply to my message. And then you didn't answer the door."

"I was going to bed. How the hell did you get in?"

"Unhooked the keys through the letterbox with a coat-hanger. You really shouldn't leave them in the lock."

"I won't anymore," Liz said, walking down the stairs. She didn't bother asking Bernie why she had a coat-hanger with her. Some things it was best not to know. "Dave's gone to drop Sean off with his grandparents for the next few days. I was looking forward to some peace and quiet."

"Well, now you have me and that's much better."

Liz's back gave a twinge and she sat down on the sofa, giving Bernie a flick of her wrist that indicated she could do the same.

"You're on the clock, Berns. Tell me what it is that you want."

"I need to run this Abbey thing by you. I know you weren't too keen on us taking the case –"

"I think you'll find that I explicitly said you shouldn't take it."

Bernie shrugged. "I thought there was room for negotiation. And besides, that was before we found out who Mrs Guthrie is."

"And who is she?"

"A real piece of work. Annabel Passer, now Guthrie. I went to school with her and she was a bully. The kind that never hit you but said things worse than a slap in the face. That sort."

"All right, I know the type. But that doesn't mean she had anything to do with her husband's murder."

"Hmmn," Bernie didn't sound convinced. "I have a pal who stays on her street and she says that there's been a police car outside her house all day, so there's probably no chance of getting in to interview her, not at the moment anyway."

"That does make things difficult," Liz said, her mind on how many nappies she should take to the hospital.

"It just means we need to look at the other angles. I've just got off the phone with the Reverend."

That made Liz pay attention. "What, at ten o'clock at night?"

Bernie rolled her eyes. "You sound just as grumpy as he did. And I will explain to you as I did to him that the needs of his parishioners are twenty-four hours a day. A good Reverend should always be available to his flock in their time of need."

"Aren't you Catholic?"

"You're splitting hairs. Anyway, I told him I was investigating the death of the stonemason. He said he wasn't even in Invergryff yesterday, which matches what Mary said."

"Did he give you anything useful?" Liz asked.

"He told me the names of the other guys doing the restoration work. He couldn't tell me if any of them were due in yesterday. It's up to the guys to set their own hours, which doesn't help the investigation much."

"I'm surprised he told you that."

"Apparently he was eager to get off the phone. I might have interrupted his bath."

"Right."

"There was something else. The Reverend was a bit... odd."

"Odd, like eccentric? Or like pushing stonemasons off the roof odd?"

Bernie picked a bit of fluff from her leggings. "He didn't sound like he liked Guthrie much. I expected him to be all 'do not speak ill of the dead' but he started going on about the man being lazy. Not turning up for shifts, that sort of thing. I just thought it was strange that he mentioned it. Of course, there's no reason to think the Reverend was involved. Except I don't trust anyone who reckons they can speak to God. And he didn't seem to have any reason to dislike our dead man, but still... definitely odd."

"You don't kill someone because they are lazy or late for their shifts."

"I wouldn't. But who's to say what our Reverend might do? I'm going to see if I can get into the Abbey tomorrow."

"Any other leads?" Liz said, beginning to get interested in spite of herself.

"Well, anyone married to that awful Annabel woman would probably be looking for a way out, so I'm wondering if there's another woman involved somewhere," Bernie suggested.

"You think he was cheating on his wife?"

"It happens. If it didn't we wouldn't have much of a business."

Liz massaged her swollen ankles. "That's true."

"You know I've often thought that the problem with marriage is that women want something to love – a kid, or an other-half of some kind – and men generally just want a ride-on lawnmower."

"But that's… Bernie, even for you that's cynical," Liz said.

"I know. Doesn't stop it being true."

Bernie grabbed some sort of runner's gel out of her bumbag and squeezed it into her mouth. "So my list of suspects so far are Mrs Guthrie, right at the top, then some unknown co-worker that we haven't met yet, then the Reverend."

"Because he sounded a bit shifty on the phone?"

"Exactly."

Liz wriggled her toes to try and ease the swelling in her feet. "I don't know, Bernie, it doesn't sound like you've got much to go on."

"Maybe I should ask Alice for advice."

The room grew a little chillier. "Ah. She came to see you, then?"

"You didn't have to be so sneaky about it," Bernie said with a sniff.

"I did. You're so proud Berns you would never have reached out. But you know as well as I do that you're going to need the help over the next few weeks."

"Maybe I will. You know you can take as long as you like for maternity leave, the WWC will cover it all."

"Just not too long, eh?" Liz gave her a wink.

"Aye, not too long. I need you around for when I have to be

nice to people. It's not my strong point."

"Mary's nice."

Bernie barked out a laugh. "She's too nice. You're the iron fist in the velvet glove. Mary's the velvet glove all right, only there's a chocolate trifle inside."

"That's a really gross image."

"Yeah. Now I better let you get some beauty sleep. You look like something the cat dragged in, then left under the bed for six months until it dissolved into the carpet."

Liz stood up and pointed to the door. "Thanks for coming, Bernie. Don't let the door hit your arse on the way out."

Chapter 9: Mary

Tuesday morning was one of those that had disaster written all over it before Mary had even woken up. By the time she had shoved the kids through the door of the school she had already dealt with a serious cereal spill, two nosebleeds and one child-toilet-related-disaster which had meant a comprehensive bleaching of an entire bathroom.

Mary had therefore been pleased when Liz had texted her to say that all the paperwork had been sent over to the interested parties in the Lochwinnoch Drive case.

She had been less pleased when Mr Biggins had rung up to shout at her five minutes later.

"You said you would get this sorted. A shared boundary with right of way? She can pull her wheelie bins right through my begonias, is that what you're saying?"

"I'm sure your solicitor can explain it all, Mr Biggins, we just passed the relevant research on to her."

"She charges me two hundred quid an hour, I'd much rather hear it from you."

"Well, you see, the boundaries were established in sixty-six when the houses were first built. However, the access to the amenities was established by your neighbour in the nineteen eighties. We found that Mrs Mackenzie was merely using what had become a de-facto right of way."

"That's all legal talk. What does that mean?"

"It means she can use the pathway through your back garden when she doesn't have an alternative. And you can't prevent her."

"She's won then? Is that it?"

"No, not at all. The same right of way means that she cannot keep her bushes so tall as they are restricting your access to the lane at the back of the house. So you get a concession too, Mr Biggins."

"Doesn't sound like it," the man grumbled. "Sounds like you're on her side. And what about my floral borders?"

Although her patience had been honed through years of dealing with toddlers, Mary beginning to feel rather frazzled. "She can't just roll her bin over them, if that's what you mean. She has a duty to return any part of the garden back to its prior state."

"That's more like it hen, I can sue her for damage to my garden?"

Mary sighed. "A few quid's worth of damage? It's not going to be worth the lawyer's fees."

"It will be if it teaches the old windbag a lesson. Do you know that she was a right stuck-up bint even in school? Looked down her nose at the likes of me because we got free school meals. Well, I'm going to show her now."

"That's great, Mr Biggins. Just please make sure you don't

keep us posted." She ended the call before he could work out what she had just said.

Mary went to make a cup of tea but before the kettle had boiled her phone started ringing again.

"Mr Biggins, I already explained —"

"I am not that odious man," Mrs Mackenzie said. Her voice was twenty per cent posher on the phone.

"I'm very sorry for the mix-up," Mary said. "How can I help you?"

"I want to complain about your outrageous report."

"Of course you do."

It took another half hour before Mary could get off the phone. Just as she did so, the doorbell rang.

"Hello Bernie," Mary said, holding the door aside to let her boss in. "I've just come off the phone with one of our clients. Actually, with two of our clients."

"Let me guess, Lochwinnoch Drive?"

"Yes. They are both mad as hell. Neither one is accepting the solicitor's documents. And they don't even pretend to be listening when I speak. Ugh, why did you give them my number," Mary said.

"Well, I could hardly give them Liz's considering her condition."

"You could have given them yours!"

Bernie chuckled. "No thanks. Look, we've made good money on this case. We just need to keep both sides sweet until they pay their final bills."

Mary opened the patio doors to the garden so that they could sit outside. The honey-sweet smell of next door's roses drifted over the fence. Invergryff summers were so short that the novelty never wore off of being able to sit in the sunshine. She brought out a jug of water and a couple of glasses.

"I went to see Liz last night," Bernie said, drinking half her glass in one go. She was wearing her tunic which meant she was going to work at the care home later. Despite having officially quit to work for the WWC full-time, Bernie hadn't quite left her previous job. She claimed that they were too short-staffed to do without her, but Mary reckoned she just missed all the gossip.

"How is she feeling?"

"Pretty god damn terrible, I'd imagine. I didn't ask. They're going to induce her tomorrow so even if she doesn't go into labour, she'll be out of the game soon. And I wanted to talk to you about how we're going to manage at the WWC."

Mary wiped a bead of condensation from the outside of her glass. In truth, she had been expecting this conversation for a while. She had joined the Wronged Women's Co-operative as nothing more than a part-time admin assistant, but over the last year that role had broadened into something deeper. Now that Liz was going off on maternity leave, it was time that Mary stepped up to the plate, and she was ready to do so.

"The thing is, I know this is a bit out of the blue, but..." Bernie glanced at her phone. "Crap, is that the time? I need to get to work."

"You can just ask me now if you like," Mary said with a smile.

"I don't think I need your permission, do I?"

A frown creased her brows. "Sorry, what are you talking about?"

"Alice. I've asked her to come back and work with us. It means that with me and you two part-timers, we should be able to cover Liz for the few weeks that she's off."

Part-timer? Mary had thought she was something more than that. She pulled her legs up on her chair. At least Bernie didn't seem to notice that she was upset. The woman's complete detachment from other people's feelings had that upside.

Bernie stood up to leave. "So we'll sort things out with Alice. I'm going to get her to check out the Abbey, see where our murderer could have got access. I want you to do the interviews."

Mary blinked. "We're taking the Abbey case?"

"Didn't I mention it? We're going to find out how Mrs Annabel Guthrie murdered her husband."

"We're going to what?"

"Must dash. Emergency WWC meeting at my place tonight, assuming Liz isn't in the hospital."

Mary was still sitting open-mouthed when she heard Bernie's car pull out of the street. She went into the kitchen and stuffed a Jaffa cake into her mouth. So Bernie still thought of her as the admin support, just like when she'd first joined up. Why had she ever imagined it would be different? Just because she had been the key person involved in what – four, five – murder cases? Not to mention any number of cheating husbands and wives. And last month, when Sir Victor Robertson's prize cat had disappeared, who had spent two days camped out in the woods in the pouring rain coaxing the damned thing out from a badger set? And had the scratches to prove it?

She pulled on her coat. It was still only ten o'clock in the morning. She would just bloody well show Bernie what she was made of. Was it Bernadette Paterson, head of the private investigation agency, who had seen the man fall to his death in the Abbey? No, it was not. It was Mary Plunkett, five foot three, lover of cake and the owner of not one, not two, but three different editions of the Buffy the Vampire Slayer DVD collection.

Mary jumped into the car and drove to the Abbey, eighties power ballads blaring out of the speakers. By the time she got parked she was ready to fight. Or interview an elderly lady. Whichever was required.

The Abbey had a sign up to say it had 'reopened after an unexpected closure' with no mention of the murder. The number of visitors, however, suggested that plenty of people had come lured by the sensation story rather than the gothic architecture. Mary headed straight for the gift shop.

"Is Mrs Button in?" Mary asked the woman behind the till who she didn't recognise.

"She's in the back sorting out the stock room," the other woman said, in between handing out flyers to tourists.

"Can you tell her Mary Plunkett wants to speak to her?"

"Sure."

The woman hurried away and returned a few moments later with Mrs Button who was today sporting a fuchsia coloured cardigan and a pair of glasses on a string. Mary found these mildly fascinating as she had never seen anyone wear them outside of an Oscar Wilde play.

"Nice to see you again, dear. Eva, I'm off on my break."

Eva didn't look too impressed as Mrs Button strolled out of the gift shop, and Mary gave her an apologetic glance on the way out.

"Eva wasn't there on Sunday, was she?" Mary asked.

"No. She's cover for the girl, Jodie, who's gone off sick. Mental health apparently. It's the new back pain, you know. Any excuse to be home with their feet up if you ask me. Now my little flat is just across the bridge over there, if we're quick we can get a cup of tea and you can ask your questions."

"My questions?"

"Oh, I know all about your investigative agency. After that terrible business on Sunday I looked you up on the web."

"We're sort of unofficially investigating this one," Mary explained. "But I knew that you would be the person to speak to if I wanted to find out what was going on at the Abbey."

"Flattery will get you everywhere," Mrs Button cackled as she led the way to a small block of flats with olive trees out in front.

Five minutes later Mary was happily seated on a sofa while Mrs Button made the tea. Little old ladies were her favourite category of person to interview. She might not have been a private investigator for long, but Mary had learned that ladies in their later years knew everything that went on, and they were happy to spill other people's secrets. And they were never shy when offering biscuits.

"Ooh, I haven't had a chocolate digestive for ages," Mary said, grabbing one off the plate.

"I don't think it is worth bothering with biscuits if they aren't chocolate coated," Mrs Button said.

"I quite agree," Mary said, munching happily. "Thank you for agreeing to speak to me. I know it must have been a difficult couple of days."

"It wasn't much fun," Mrs Button said, with an eager expression that told Mary that she wasn't being entirely honest. "Seeing poor Alexander fall like that... well, it was dreadful."

"You didn't actually see the fall though, did you? I thought you were in the gift shop at the time."

"Ah yes, well, it feels like I was there. And, of course, we heard it. That terrible thump he made as he hit the floor. I shall never forget it."

"Neither will I," Mary agreed. "Now, the police haven't said it's definitely murder yet, but we think there's a good chance someone else was involved."

"I've been thinking about that all day," Mrs Button said. "It is possible that someone else was up there. Especially if they came in through the roof."

"It would be possible to do that?"

She nodded. "Oh yes. There's plenty of ways up if you know the Abbey. There's a door that leads right into the central area. That would take you to the scaffolding where poor Alexander was working."

"I suppose that means that only someone who knew their way around the Abbey could have killed them. Someone that worked there and knew that they could escape the same way."

"Could be. But we've had a lot of vandalism too over the years. Someone stole a whole load of lead from one of the lower roofs in the nineties. Not to mention the kids with their spray paint."

Mary deflated a little. "Are you saying that there are more people that know their way around the Abbey than we think?"

"I'm afraid so. Although I can't see why some young vandal would kill Alexander. Unless he surprised them in the act and it was an accident."

Check out vandalism angle, Mary wrote in her notepad.

"Did Alexander ever fall out with anyone at the Abbey? A row with a boss, that sort of thing."

"He didn't really have a boss. The stonemasons didn't need supervision, they just got on with their work and every couple of months the committee would take a look at it. Old Mr Smail kept an eye on the day to day stuff, not that it took much effort."

"Old Mr Smail?" Mary said with a small smile.

Mrs Button leaned over and gave Mary a smack on the knee. "I know what you're thinking lass, but there's old and there's *old*. That Mr Smail has been old since he was about fifty. Bad hip, dicky ticker, the works. I might have a few years on him but I'm never at the doctors. Once you start thinking of yourself as an old bugger, that's when you're done for."

"Noted. There was no trouble with the other stonemasons, then? No fallouts there?"

"Alexander was good friends with Sam Finlayson. That's the older guy that he apprenticed under. There was no bad blood there. And he seemed to get on well with Cammie too. That's the younger lad. They were both learning from Sam, although he'd not long come back to work. You know, his wife was killed in that bad car crash last year. The Abbey gave him compassionate leave. It was really sad."

"What crash was that?"

"She came off the road up in the Braes. It was on the news at the time. They didn't find the car until the next day. Poor man. I don't like to repeat gossip, but the story was that she was driving home drunk. She was only forty-five. And now his workmate's dead. Poor soul."

Mary felt a pang of sympathy for the man. Bad enough that his wife had been killed without the whole place gossiping about her drinking after her death. She made a mental note to ask Walker about the car crash the next time she saw him.

"What about the Reverend?"

She noted that for the first time Mrs Button looked like she didn't want to reply.

"There was no trouble there, I'm sure."

"Is there something about Reverend McDade that's worrying you?"

Mrs Button barked out a laugh. "Nothing to do with Alexander's death. I just don't like his attitude. He's one of these new Christians that we're always hearing about. Spends too much time on his laptop rather than in the pulpit, if you ask me. But then no one does, so what does it matter?"

Mary wanted to probe further, but Mrs Button pushed off the arms of her chair and got to her feet.

"I better get back to work. You will call if you need anything else."

"I will," Mary said, and she meant it. There was something that Mrs Button wasn't telling her about the Reverend and she wanted to find out what.

Chapter 10: Walker

Walker was co-ordinating the door-knockers. Normally, that would be the people going around the neighbours to see if they'd seen anything suspicious. The problem in this case was that the crime scene was the Abbey, so half of the town were the neighbours. Normally, they were glad to have CCTV for any crime, but in this case they had more than they could handle. By Tuesday morning, two days after the death of Alexander Guthrie, most of the Constables in Invergryff police station were still sat staring at grainy black and white footage on their laptop screens.

At ten o'clock he walked up to the front of the incident room to give a summary of what they had found so far. He was feeling a little nervous, as he had tried to make notes but that wasn't his strong point. Luckily the images on the screen spoke for themselves.

"We'll start with when Alexander Guthrie arrives for work on Sunday morning," he said, clicking the laptop so that the first image came up of a man in overalls heading through the main door of the Abbey. "The time on the CCTV is seven forty-five. The guys working on the building liked to arrive early so they could finish up by the afternoon. This was confirmed by Mr Smail. He was already there by this point as he started opening up at seven."

"The two women arrive to work in the gift shop by half eight, then the Abbey opens to the public at nine. After that, at least two hundred people come through in the next few hours."

Macleod groaned. "What a nightmare."

Walker nodded in agreement. "The guys are working on making sure that all of those people that came in, also came back out, but as you can imagine it's going to take some time."

"What about the people that didn't come in through the front door?" Macleod asked.

"That's the trickier bit," Walker explained. "There's not any CCTV that we can find that gives us a good view of the roof. There's a chance we might catch something on one of the shop systems, but it's looking unlikely. We've put out a call for witnesses, so there's a chance that someone might have seen someone climbing up there. But if that's how our killer got up there, we've not much chance of getting any footage of them."

"All right, what about inside the Abbey?"

Walker wished he could have given the DI some better news. "There is CCTV. It's pointed at the gift shop exit. Luckily we've got a couple of pics of Guthrie as the sign-in sheet is just past there. So we have him signing in at seven forty-five, signing out for lunch at twelve and back in half an hour later. And we know that time of death was at one-forty-seven."

"Thanks to our intrepid lad on the scene who took a note of the time," Macleod said, gesturing to Walker to sit down.

"Do we know where he went for lunch?"

"No. And there's something interesting about that. Neil, have you got the list of the victim's possessions."

Sergeant Neil Michelson passed over the document. Walker scanned it carefully. Yes, there it was.

"It says here that he had in his backpack a ham sandwich and a packet of crisps, uneaten. That sounds like lunch to me."

"Interesting," Macleod rubbed his chin. "He went out for lunch even though he'd brought it with him. Could suggest he was meeting someone?"

"That's what I thought, sir."

"Or it could be that he just fancied some chips. Get the guys on the CCTV to have another look around twelve, see if they can work out where he went. And get someone around to the local cafes, see if anyone saw him that day."

Macleod downed a cup of coffee, wincing at the taste. "Those vending machines get worse every time I come down here. Anyway, I wanted to go through these post-mortem results while I have you all here. Doctor Catto did the PM first thing this morning. It confirms our initial findings that Guthrie's death was not natural. The Doctor can't confirm if he was dead or not before he hit the ground, but the head wound definitely happened pre-mortem and would have contributed to his death. The wound is consistent with the trowel that Sergeant Walker found at the crime scene, and DNA from Guthrie was found on the trowel. Sadly no fingerprints on the weapon, or any prints on the scaffolding apart from the three stonemasons. But our suspect could have used gloves."

"For the moment, until we find evidence of the involvement of anyone else, I want to focus on the other two men that Guthrie was working with. That's Sam Finlayson and Paul Cameron, known as Cammie. Finlayson doesn't have a record, but Neil did some digging on Paul Cameron this morning."

At the DI's nod, Neil stood up and cleared his throat. "He's never been in trouble up here, but it looks like he left England under a bit of a cloud. There was a bar fight a year ago, two lads badly beaten up, one of them ended up in a coma. Cameron was looking at aggravated assault, but his defence got it shot down. Word is from the local station that he went after the lads with a half-brick, but they couldn't prove it was him and not one of the boys he was with. He got a sympathetic jury and got away with affray and a suspended sentence.

There was a murmur around the room directed at soft-hearted juries.

"He's a man with a temper, that we know," Macleod says. "So I reckon we want to ask him some questions. According to Mr Smail at the Abbey, it was his day off, but as we've heard their security wasn't exactly watertight and he could have sneaked in."

"More likely to be someone with inside knowledge," Neil said. "I mean, I wouldn't be chancing fighting someone up on that scaffolding if I wasn't very sure of where I was standing."

Macleod nodded. "Aye, I think you're right. Could be that Cameron or Finlayson turned up, had an argument with our man and bashed his head in. Then they scarpered over the roof."

"It's going to be hard to prove if it is one of the two stonemasons," Walker said, thinking out loud. "Their prints and DNA will be all over the place anyway."

"Thanks for your optimism, Sergeant," Macleod barked back, but he softened his words with a rueful smile. They all could see how tricky this was going to be to take to court. "Let's get Mr Cameron and Mr Finlayson in for questioning today and see where that gets us."

Walker barely had time to finish typing up his notes when Macleod walked over to his desk and rapped his knuckles on the table.

"Want to sit in on the interview with Finlayson? He's on his way over right now. I like a suspect that's punctual."

"Sure."

Walker tried hard not to look too keen. Normally it would be a non-uniform member of the Major Investigation Team doing the interview, so for Macleod to ask him to come in with him was a good sign. He was hoping to ask for a transfer to plain clothes soon, but it was important to get the timing right. Walker didn't want to seem impatient or overconfident and harm his chances of becoming a detective.

"I'll just grab a chocolate bar on the way down," Macleod said as they reached the stairs. "Wouldn't want to get hangry now would I?"

When I'm a detective I'm going to eat better than that, Walker promised himself, watching his boss tear off the wrapper and chomp into the chocolate. Mind you, it did look good.

"Right, I'll handle the questions, but feel free to jump in if you think of anything. We'll frame it like we're trying to get a picture of the deceased. I don't want to formally arrest him and start the clock ticking until we've got some evidence."

Walker just had time to take all this in before they went into the interview room.

Finlayson was one of those older guys who had kept his muscle but got leaner with age. He had well-tanned skin from working outside and a beanie hat pulled down over a bald head.

He looked nervous, but then most people did in a police station.

Walker busied himself with sorting out the 'tape' – a compact disk, the police service might move to digital sometime in the present millennium – and making sure that the interview formalities were met. Once everyone had identified themselves, Macleod could start the questions.

"Thank you for coming so promptly, Mr Finlayson. This is an informal interview and you are free to leave at any time."

"I wanted to get the record straight."

Macleod's eyebrows flickered upwards. "And what do you mean by that?"

The builder traced a line on the table with his finger. "I know you'll be looking into AJ's records. His bank account, that sort of thing. And I wanted to explain something."

Walker almost smiled. It wasn't often that people offered themselves forward as suspects, but that was exactly what Finlayson appeared to be up to.

"The thing is, I owed him a bit of cash. I want to tell you that now, before you go hunting around and find it out. Just over two grand."

Not a massive amount of cash, but the sad fact was that Walker knew that plenty of men had been killed for less.

"And why was that?" Macleod asked.

"I was behind on the mortgage. Not by much, but once you get behind it's hard to catch up, and I was off work for a while after my wife died."

"In a car crash, is that right?"

Finlayson nodded, his lips pressed together in a thin line.

"AJ was good to me after my wife passed away. He was the one that convinced me to come back to work. And he lent me that money until I paid off the arrears on the mortgage. I'd already paid a grand back to him since last month, and I was going to do the same on Friday when my wages came in. So that's why I wanted to explain. I was paying him the money back. We were friends, and he was… a good pal."

The man's grief seemed genuine, but he could just have been a good actor.

"Can you go over your movements on Sunday for us," Macleod said.

"It was my day off. I was at home. And no, since my wife died I have no one to vouch for me. I didn't even know that AJ was dead until Jodie from the gift shop texted me. I phoned up Henry Smail to check. I couldn't believe it. Of course, I thought it was an accident. Are you sure it wasn't? It's a dangerous job. I know a few lads that have been killed coming off roofs."

"At the moment we are treating it as a suspicious death," Macleod said. "Did you notice anything unusual about Mr Guthrie in the last few weeks? Any changes in his behaviour?"

"Nothing. He seemed a happy lad. Mind you, he wasn't the type to moan about things. He just got on with the job. Same as when he'd been my apprentice."

"What about his personal life? His marriage?"

Finlayson shrugged. "As I said, he never really talked about it. I did wonder if there was a reason they never had kids, but you don't like to ask about these things. Same as me and my wife. It just never happened."

Macleod looked to Walker to see if there was anything else.

"What about the other guy you work with? Paul Cameron."

"I don't know him that well. He came up from down south. Does some of the more specialised stuff."

"Mr Guthrie's wife told us that he was jealous of the money

that Cameron was making."

A frown flickered across Finlayson's face. "Did she? I suppose he might have been, but the specialist guys are always paid more. And as I said, AJ was happy to lend me the cash for my mortgage, no questions asked."

"So you never had the feeling he was tight with his cash?"

"Definitely not. The opposite, in fact. As I said, he was a good bloke."

Finlayson left the interview room with his head bowed low. The police officers sat in silence for a while, Macleod flicking through the file folder and collecting his thoughts.

"It doesn't quite match up, does it? The wife told us he was tight, that he hated giving out money. Now Finlayson tells us he was happy to lend money around. Someone's not telling us the truth there."

"Should we speak to the wife again?" Walker asked.

"Not yet. I'd rather go back when we've got something more concrete to challenge her with. Let's take a look into the victim's bank records, see if Finlayson is telling the truth about the loan."

"All right," Walker said, making a note on his phone. "What's next?"

"We go back to the CCTV. Check that Finlayson doesn't pop up on it. And let's see if we can get permission to do a location check on his phone for Sunday too. If he moved out of his house then I want to know about it."

"What about his reason for killing Guthrie? It seems unlikely that he'd kill his mate for a two grand loan, especially if he was paying it back."

"Motives are for detectives on the telly, Walker. Let's focus on the evidence for now."

Chastened, Walker followed Macleod back to the office, stopping at the vending machine for a chocolate pick-me-up as he did so.

Chapter 11: Bernie

It wasn't until after lunch on Tuesday that Bernie worked out how she was going to get a way in with Annabel Guthrie. She had exhausted all of her contacts. Every member of the care home had been canvassed to see if any knew either of the Guthrie's but she had drawn a blank.

It was the cleaners that came up trumps, as they so often did. It had occurred to Bernie that Annabel was probably the sort of person who didn't like to scrub her own loo. Sure enough, when she asked her friend Mira from the home, the network of Polish cleaners got to texting each other and it turned out that a woman called Julia cleaned the Guthrie's house every second Friday.

Julia could be bribed for as little as a cup of tea and a pastry in a café in the East End of town where Bernie had gone to meet her after her shift.

"I can only stay for five minutes," the woman said. "I have to get back for Bargain Hunt."

"That's fine," Bernie said, happy to be brief. "I want to know about your client, Mrs Annabel Guthrie, the one whose husband just died."

The pastry was disappearing piece by piece into Julia's mouth. "I like her. She tidies up before I come. Not everyone does that."

"Huh." This was not what Bernie wanted to hear. "But I bet she makes nasty remarks, criticises you, that sort of thing."

Julia sniffed. "Like when you told me how much saturated fat was in this pastry?"

"That was just factual information. Did Annabel Guthrie ever bully you?"

"Bully? No, she paid on time, she didn't give me too much work. I liked her. She even sent me a message to cancel this Friday when her poor husband died."

"Her husband dies and her first thought is to message the cleaner? Seems a little chilly."

"She is very organised. Nothing wrong with that."

"What about her husband, did you ever meet him?"

"Only once. He came back to the house to get something he forgot. He was usually out at work before I arrived."

"And you didn't sense any trouble in their marriage?"

A flake of pastry fell onto the table. "No."

Bernie pounced on the pause before Julia uttered another word. "You did see something, didn't you?"

Julia was not a small woman and when she squirmed her whole upper half trembled. "I do not want to get anyone in trouble."

"Of course you don't. But sometimes you must do the right thing, even if there is trouble. And I'll personally make sure that it doesn't come back to you."

"I hear they do the pastries for takeaway as well."

Bernie sighed. It was tough when your methods became known around town. "All right, there's a box of six going home with you."

"That time that Mr Guthrie came home early, I was in the house by myself. It was a few weeks ago, around half past nine because I had just started on the upstairs. He let himself in and I hadn't heard him. I came downstairs and he had a laptop open in the study. When he saw me he slammed it shut. He seemed really flustered, then he grabbed his wallet and left."

"Uh huh. And what was he looking at on the laptop?"

"I have no idea."

"You're trying to tell me you didn't peek?"

Julia's mouth turned up at the corner. "All right, I opened it up to take a look. I assumed it would be porn, because, you know…"

"He's a man," Bernie nodded.

"But it was just a map of the town. You know, like an online thing where you put in directions. And he was looking at some random streets outside Invergryff. I just thought it was a weird thing to be so secretive about."

It wasn't exactly an affair, but at least it was something. "Can you write me down the streets you remember from the map?"

Julia stood up. "I will try. I will send them in a text message. I need to get back…"

"To Bargain Hunt, yes I know."

After she left, Bernie sipped her black coffee. The crumbs of pastry littered the table like confetti. It wasn't so very long ago that Bernie herself would have been devouring pastries and cakes like Julia had. Oh, people thought she was obsessive about food, and maybe she was, but Bernie knew where it got you. It wasn't her size that was the issue. It was using food as emotional comfort. No one except for Bernie would ever understand the effort it had taken to reset her body as she had done. People like Annabel Guthrie who had made her feel so much shame when she had been chubby – but not anything like as big as she became later on – had made things so much worse. When others hated you, it was easy to start hating yourself, and that's what had happened to the old Bernie.

Maybe the new Bernie was a little tough, but that was what she had needed to be. If Annabel Guthrie had never existed then maybe Bernie could have learned to show a little weakness. She put down her cup and pulled on her coat. That ship had sailed, but there was still time to get even with her tormentor. Never mind what Julia had said, she was determined to find out how Annabel had killed her husband, and why.

The new Bernie never shirked from confrontation, and that was why she left the café and arrived at the Guthries' house a few minutes later. There was one tiny problem with her plan and that was the police car parked outside.

Even Bernie realised that this was not the time to come up

against the cops. When she had her proof that Mrs Guthrie was the killer, that would be when she would swan up to the police station and solve their murder for them. For now, she resolved to leave it alone.

Until, that was, she saw Annabel Guthrie sneak out of her own front garden and start walking down the street. Twenty-something years later but Bernie would have recognised her anywhere. She had changed her blond pigtails for a sleek blond bob and she was wearing a raincoat pulled around her body even though the sun was shining. Her face was blotchy as if she had been crying, but Bernie reckoned that could easily be shame from committing murder rather than genuine sadness. Before she could think about it, she had already climbed out of the car.

"Mrs Guthrie? I'm very sorry for your loss, have you got a minute?"

Annabel flinched when she saw Bernie walking towards her.

"I don't want to talk right now," she said and sure enough, it was the same clipped tone that Bernie remembered.

"I understand that, I just wanted to ask you a couple of questions."

"Bloody hell, I just wanted to have a cigarette in peace," Annabel said, "without the family liaison woman breathing down my neck."

For a moment, Bernie felt a pang of sympathy for the woman. Then she remembered the time that pretty little Bella had thrown her new trainers into the disabled loo. The whole school had called Bernie 'poo shoes' for about a month.

"I need to ask you some questions," Bernie repeated.

"Are you a journalist? The police said they would keep them away."

That settled it: Annabel didn't recognise her. Of course she didn't. Bernie was literally half the person she used to be. This was just perfect.

"Yeah, you found me out. I work for one of the local papers. I guess we were hoping to get your side of the story."

"I have nothing to say."

"Right. So you don't feel the need to refute any of the accusations going around then."

"Accusations?"

"It'll all be in the evening edition," Bernie said, not sure if papers even had evening editions anymore. "You can read it then."

"You'll tell me right now," Mrs Guthrie told her and the steely tone was vintage Annabel Passer.

"We've been looking into your marriage, Mrs Guthrie."

Something flashed across her face, but it wasn't fear. Bernie wasn't entirely sure, but she thought it might be relief.

"My marriage was perfectly fine. I don't know what you're

planning on printing, but if you tell these lies I will take you to court."

Not an affair then, Bernie thought. The woman was too sure of herself. She decided to try another tactic. "It's not me, it's my editor. He's looking for an angle on this case. He knows that your husband's death wasn't an accident and he's going to print something."

Mrs Guthrie lit her cigarette and blew out a puff of blue smoke. "Maybe they should look elsewhere. The police have been questioning some of Alex's colleagues. If they suspected me then they wouldn't be doing that, would they?"

Bernie pretended to play along. "Which of those colleagues do you think is the most suspicious?"

Mrs Guthrie shrugged. "I'm not doing your job for you, but if I were you I'd look into that Paul Cameron. Alexander never liked him."

"Right, thanks for that," Bernie said, plastering on a fake smile. "Look, I'll see what I can do with the boss, okay?"

Mrs Guthrie just glared at her.

"Oh, and you know that as well as causing cancer, smoking is terribly bad for your skin. Something to think about, eh?"

Bernie turned on her heel before Mrs Guthrie could say anything else. Just as she did so, her phone buzzed with a message from Alice.

Don't go near Annabel Guthrie!

Bernie clicked the phone off. Was Alice psychic or had she been spotted? It hardly mattered. She had achieved what she had gone there for. Annabel Guthrie was hiding something. Maybe she hadn't thrown her husband off that scaffolding, but she was involved somehow. Bernie was sure of it.

Chapter 12: Liz

Liz had spent half the day annoyed with Bernie ringing her when it was nearly baby time, then the other half of the day wishing that her friend would phone again just to alleviate the boredom. Her hospital bag was packed, Dave was on high alert for a call and Sean was with her mother. And still there was no sign of the baby coming.

She had managed to do a little work. Mary had texted her to ask if she could find out the home addresses of Guthrie and his co-workers, which was just the sort of mindless task that suited her at the moment. All her spreadsheets were up-to-date and she just had to make sure that Bernie didn't mess with any of them while she was off.

The kitchen was calling her, but Liz knew she was just bored, not hungry. If she did end up with a C-section, which was looking increasingly more likely, she wouldn't be allowed to eat anything anyway. So maybe she should just grab another biscuit while she could.

The doorbell rang and she walked over to open it, wondering if it might be Bernie with some news. Instead, there was a young woman with a blue tunic on.

"Hello, I'm your community midwife here for a wee pre-birth meeting."

"Oh. That's right, come on in." Liz had completely forgotten that she had asked for a midwife to come to the house. At the time she had thought it would be easier than dragging herself into the doctor's surgery, but now she was regretting it. Hopefully the woman wouldn't mind the dirty dishes still sitting in the sink or the open packet of biscuits on the living room table.

"I've just got to do some last minute checks so we can get you all sorted for your new arrival," the woman said. She had a girlish voice, and was one of those enthusiastic, chatty people that Liz always found draining.

"Sure," Liz replied, easing herself onto the sofa.

"How are you today?"

"Oh, huge, tired, and fed up, but apart from that, fine."

The woman's smile faltered slightly. "But you're coping okay?"

Liz resisted the urge to point out that she didn't have much of a choice. "Yes, fine."

"First of all, can I check if you have written your birthing plan?"

Liz was trying her very best not to be judgemental, but whether it was the hormones, or the preppy upbeat nature of the midwife who looked barely out of her teens, it was a struggle.

"I've not got it written down, but I'm going for an induction, and if there's no baby within twelve hours then it's a planned C-section."

Did the midwife just wrinkle her nose? Liz was certain that

she had.

"I see. I know you had a section last time, but you wouldn't consider trying a little longer for a vaginal birth this time? There's nothing to say it's not possible."

Was there any more unpleasant-sounding word than vaginal? Liz wondered. It had surely been made up by a man.

"I'm quite happy with my section," Liz said firmly. Sean's birth had been less than fun, and when the doctor had mentioned that this baby was lying in a difficult position, Liz had been more than happy to avoid the two-day 'normal' labour that she had suffered the first time.

There was definitely another nose-wrinkle. Maybe the midwife was one of those 'natural birth' people. From what Liz remembered of labour it hadn't felt very bloody natural at the time.

"Let's move on to your general health. Are you eating well, looking after yourself?"

Two sets of eyes flickered to the biscuit packet.

"Yes," Liz replied, daring the woman to question her.

All of a sudden, the midwife put her hand over her mouth, turned her head and let out the loudest sneeze.

"Sorry, I have terrible hay fever at the moment."

Ah. That might explain the nose wrinkle. Perhaps Liz was being a little harsh on the woman. It wasn't her fault that she sounded like a cheerleader from a bad romantic comedy.

"Is there anything that's worrying you? Anything I can help with?"

Liz stared at her. "No."

"Are you sure?"

All of a sudden, Liz felt a bit wobbly. "I just... sorry, I feel like I've forgotten everything from the first time. My oldest is ten and…" Oh god, she wasn't going to cry, was she?

The midwife reached over and put an arm around her shoulders. "You've done it before, you can do it again. Honestly, labour is just a day or two out of the rest of your life as a mum. I'm sure you'll be brilliant."

The midwife handed her a tissue and Liz sniffed gratefully. Lord, if Bernie could see her now it would be Liz Okoro that would be the 'wet lettuce', not Mary for once.

"What a mess," Liz said, offering the woman a watery smile. "Sorry about all this."

"You know you don't have to be strong all the time," the midwife said and that was it, Liz was off again.

By the time she had ushered the midwife out of the door, Liz had gone through half a box of tissues. Once she managed to get her breath back she reached into the cupboard and brought out the box of chocolates that someone had left for her at the baby shower. They were for the birth, which was why she was carefully replacing the plastic wrap every time she nicked another one out of it.

She popped a strawberry crème into her mouth and grabbed her phone. "Bernie, you've got to give me something to do," she said as soon as her friend answered.

"I thought you didn't approve of me taking this case."

"I don't. And I still think it's a terrible idea. But if I don't have something to take my mind off this baby I'm going to go insane. It's either that or I ring my mother to come round just so I have someone to talk to."

"Good Lord, don't do that. I'll think of something for you." Liz could hear Bernie typing away on her laptop. "All right, have you still got your contacts in finance handy?"

Liz grinned. "The ones who don't mind breaking the odd GDPR law? Yes."

"Great. I want as much money stuff as you can find on Mr and Mrs Guthrie. At first, I thought she had killed him because she was having an affair, but that's looking less likely. So it must be money. I don't suppose you can get their bank statements?"

"That might be a little tricky, but I can get my contact to take a dig around their credit files."

"Excellent."

"I'll check out the other suspects too. We still don't have any good reason for it being the wife."

"Apart from knowing that she has the soul of a criminal?" Bernie snapped back. "While you're at it, would you look into the Reverend's accounts for me? I still think there was something weird about him."

"Understood." If the midwife had loosened her up a little, Bernie's call had energised her. Liz needed that reminder that she was more than just a soon-to-be-vacated womb.

She opened up her laptop and started to do some mildly illegal investigating.

Chapter 13: Mary

It was heading for dinner time when Mary got a call that she needed to head over to Bernie's place. After reminding Bernie that she had four kids at home and no one to watch them, they compromised. This meant that twenty minutes later Bernie turned up with a handy babysitter in the form of her niece, Jackie, and a chippy tea for the kids.

"Could you chop up some fresh veg to go with the chips?" Mary asked Jackie who had already got to work at the table on the patio laying out plastic plates and forks.

"Mum guilt?" Bernie asked.

"It would make life easier if you gave me a bit more notice," Mary said, as close as she would come to directly criticising the woman.

"Crime doesn't wear a watch," Bernie said in a patronising tone.

Mary collected the children and Jackie sat down with them outside so that they could have some peace.

"Now that the kids are out of the way I need to update you on the Abbey case," Bernie explained. "Mrs Guthrie was putting on a great show of being upset, but I'm sure that she's faking it."

"You went to see his wife? Are you sure that was a good

idea?"

"If I waited for a good idea to come along I'd never get anything done. I wanted to see the whites of her eyes. Annabel Passer. She might have changed her name but I know the nasty little bully is still in there."

"What did she say to you?"

"Nothing you could put your finger on," Bernie brushed a hair from her eyes. "But I know she was putting on a front. She might have the police fooled, but I know what she's about."

It was strange to see Bernie so defensive. Mary decided not to push it: for all she knew, Annabel Guthrie was just as bad as Bernie thought. After all, it wasn't like they were overrun with alternative suspects for the Abbey murder, and wives generally had some sort of reason to bump off their husbands.

"What happened when you went to see her?"

"I told her I was a journalist, that there were rumours going around about her having an affair. She shot that one down pretty quickly. But there was definitely something going on in that marriage, I'm just not sure what. I'll need to speak to her again, but not yet. All that one earned me was a right telling-off from Alice. Why I ever agreed to let her back in the WWC is beyond me."

"Because we're short-staffed," Mary said, not adding that Bernie had been clear about not wanting to rely on the *part-timers*.

"The sooner Liz pops out this baby the better. Any news yet?"

"None. I'll put the kettle on," Mary said. "Then I can tell you about what Mrs Button told me before we head out."

While they drank their tea, Mary explained to Bernie what the lady from the gift shop had said about the two men that Alexander Guthrie worked with.

"Doesn't sound like either of them have much of a motive," Bernie said. "But we'll keep digging. Oh, I nearly forgot, I've brought around a packet of lentil chips for you. I've got loads at home and they're high in protein."

"You're okay, I've already eaten," Mary said quickly. In fact, she had nicked a handful of chips from the kids' plates when no one was looking.

Bernie opened a cupboard. "I'll just pop them in here for you for later, shall I? Oh look, there's a packet already in there. Are these the ones from the last time I came?"

"I don't suppose you've got any other suspects in the Abbey case?" Mary said, handing Bernie her a fresh cup of tea and leading her out of the kitchen.

"I'm working on it. I mean, I know who suspect number one is, but I need to speak to the others too."

Mary picked up two schoolbags and half a satsuma skin so that there was somewhere for them to sit. She pretended not to notice that Bernie gave the sofa a wipe with a hanky before she sat down.

"I keep thinking about that poor man. What a horrible way to die," Mary said.

"I see worse every day at the care home," Bernie said, and Mary knew she was probably right. At least death had come quickly for Alexander Guthrie.

"How is Sergeant Walker? I suppose being on this case will help with his ambitions for CID?"

Mary narrowed her eyes. "Bernie, in the six months me and Walker have been together, you have never once asked how he is."

"You're right," Bernie said with a shrug. "I don't particularly care. But I want to know if you're going to tattle-tale on me to your boyfriend after we do this interview."

"What interview?"

"We're going to go and speak to Cammie, the stonemason who worked with our victim. I still think Mrs Guthrie is the one to blame, but there's no way she climbed up on that scaffolding herself."

"You think she got someone to murder her husband for her? Isn't that a bit far-fetched?"

"No. Not if you know the woman."

It was funny, Mary had never seen Bernie behave irrationally before. Sneaky, yes, and irritating, always. But this grudge she was holding against Annabel Guthrie was something else.

"You don't think that you're letting the past influence your present a little too much," Mary suggested.

"Did you hear that on Oprah?"

"Might have been Judge Judy."

"I know people," Bernie said firmly. "And I know Annabel Guthrie. She is a bully and a snob and just the sort of person to get rid of a husband that she decided she didn't like anymore."

"All right. But if we find evidence for someone else, will you at least consider it?"

"Of course. As long as you consider ignoring your boyfriend when he tells you to stay away from this case."

Mary bit her lip. Bernie's words had reminded her how angry she'd been when Walker had dismissed her from the Abbey. "He's my boyfriend, not my keeper. I can do what I like."

"Excellent. And now you can do what *I* like and drive us over to the Cameron house."

As usual, Bernie got her way. Mary barely had time to check the kids had eaten something and show Jackie where they kept the toothbrushes before Bernie pulled her out of the door. She drove the two of them to the north side of town where there was a new housing development. The houses had that pristine white render that always looked amazing until it had been subjected to a couple of years of Scottish weather.

"This is it," Mary said, double-checking the address on the message that Liz had sent.

"Just like at the Guthrie place. Half-finished jobs everywhere.

My Finn would be like that too if I didn't keep him straight."

Mary had forgotten that Bernie's husband was a roofer.

"Did Finn know Alexander Guthrie?"

Bernie shook her head. "Not really. I asked him right after the murder. He knew the older man, Finlayson a little, just from working a few of the same jobs, but he said he only knew Guthrie to see. And he's never met this Cameron bloke."

Mary and Bernie dodged their way around the discarded bags of gravel and planks of wood and made their way to the front door. There was no doorbell so Mary reached over and banged the letterbox a couple of times.

The door was opened by a young girl around three years old who was clutching an animal soft toy that might have once been a rabbit or a bear but was no longer identifiable.

"Hi there, is your Daddy home?"

"He's at work. Do you like dinosaurs?"

"Yes," Mary said, confident in her answer. "Velociraptor is my favourite."

The girl nodded. "He could disavowel people with his claws."

"He could."

They spent a moment appreciating this fact, and then Bernie said. "Could you get your mum for us?"

The little girl just blinked. "I read a book about a princess and a dragon."

"Was it good?"

"No." The girl scratched her chin. "Who are you anyway?"

"Well, lucky for you, it turns out that I'm a princess," Mary said.

The little girl tilted her head to one side. "Don't look like a princess."

"Oh, princesses can look like anything these days."

"Spare us the feminism and get us inside," Bernie muttered.

The girl took a step backwards. "Is that the wicked witch?"

Thankfully before Bernie could answer, the front door was pulled open fully and a woman stood behind the child.

"Sorry, didn't hear you knock. Sophia wasn't bothering you, was she?"

"Not at all. She's completely adorable," Mary said, knowing that the best way to win over a mother was to compliment her children.

Sure enough, the other woman smiled so that dimples formed in her cheeks.

"We're from a private investigation agency," Bernie explained. "We'd like to talk to you about the death of Alexander Guthrie."

That wiped the smile from her face. "I didn't know him that well. He worked with Cammie, but I only met him a couple of times."

"Is Cammie in?"

"No. He won't be back from work for another half hour or so."

"Just time for a cup of tea before he turns up then," Bernie said, stepping into the hall as Mrs Marshall moved out of the way.

Mary gave her a sympathetic smile on her way past. It wasn't fair, really, to let Bernie loose on unsuspected individuals, but it did get results. Mary knew if she had asked to come in herself, she would have been told exactly where to go, but there was something about Bernie that made it impossible to argue with her.

"You said that you met Guthrie a few times," Bernie said.

"I drop Cammie at work sometimes if I need the car. And I went into the Abbey once to see the restoration. It's going to be amazing when it's done."

"Just like this place will be," Bernie said. "I notice he's working on the garden."

"The landlord hadn't done much with it and we wanted to put decking in. But we might not bother now. We're just renting this place, you see. Cammie's looking for work back down South. My mum is still down there and Sophia misses her something rotten."

Mary nodded. "I moved back here to be near my mum. It's such a help with the kids."

Alyssa Cameron gave Mary a grateful look. She preferred the good cop rather than the bad cop glowering in the corner.

"No other reason to move with a little one?" Bernie asked. "It's a lot of upheaval to move twice in such a short time."

Unless her friend was psychic, Mary reckoned that had been a shot in the dark, but Alyssa's cheeks turned pink.

"Why would there be?"

"Oh, just silly rumours," Mary said, taking the opportunity to stick the knife in. Never trust the good cop.

"If people can't move on from one mistake then that's their problem. This was meant to be a new start." The woman had turned away and started to sort out the massive pile of washing.

"What exactly did –" Just as Bernie stepped closer the front door banged open.

"Whose car is out front?" A man's voice shouted, and he didn't sound very happy.

A man in overalls walked into the room. Paul Cameron wasn't much taller than his wife, but he had broad shoulders and muscular arms. Mary felt very small all of a sudden.

"These woman wanted to ask you some questions about Alexander Guthrie."

Cameron glared at them and Mary knew they were in trouble.

"Are you with the police?" he asked.

"No," Bernie said, standing up and folding her arms. "We are private investigators."

"Then I've no reason to speak to you. Why the hell did you let them in, Alyssa? I've just wasted half my morning with the police, I'm not going to spend the rest of the day answering stupid questions. Get out of my house."

He slammed a fist against the countertop, making all the women jump. Mary didn't like the look of the man's face either. A vein at his temple was throbbing and his neck was turning red.

"Let's go Bernie. It's nearly time to pick the kids up anyway."

"We'll be back," Bernie said, in a way that would have intimidated Sarah Connor in the nineties, but seemed to have little effect on Paul Cameron. The man seemed just a few degrees away from exploding. Mary tugged Bernie on the arm and ushered them out of the house.

"Wow," Mary said when they made it back into the car. "That guy has some serious anger issues. Do you reckon he did it?"

"Maybe if they had an argument, he lost it in the moment and pushed Guthrie off the scaffolding? Yeah, I could see that. But we know that this was a planned murder, otherwise why would he have avoided signing in or appearing on the CCTV? I'm not ruling him out, but unless your boyfriend comes up with some good evidence, he's still in the middle of the pile of suspects."

"He's top for me," Mary said with a shudder. "I thought he was going to throttle us. Well, throttle you at least, Bernie. Do you never worry that you might push someone a bit too far?"

"Nope."

Mary glanced back at the house, but someone had shut the blinds. She made a note on her phone to give her a friend of hers who was a social worker a little call later. It might be nothing, but a temper like that wasn't something she liked to see around a child.

Never mind what Bernie said, she was going to get Liz to have a close look at Paul Cameron's past. It was easy enough to imagine a man like that pushing someone to their death. She closed her eyes and heard the thud as Alexander Guthrie's body hit the floor of the Abbey. Paul Cameron was capable of that, she was sure of it.

Chapter 14: Walker

Sergeant Walker was not having a brilliant afternoon. He had gone out to interview the woman in charge of the gift shop at the Abbey, but as Mrs Button explained:

"I've already told everything to that lovely investigator woman. And I'm afraid she's had all the chocolate biscuits."

Walker had sent a slightly snippy text to his girlfriend that he instantly regretted. Their respective jobs had come into conflict before, but this was the first time that he had felt like it could have a real impact on his career. DI Macleod had made his feelings very clear on the WWC, and Walker couldn't afford to challenge them.

And yet, he hated the idea of falling out with Mary. They had worked incredibly hard to get to a point where the relationship was working well for both of them. It wasn't exactly easy. Walker hadn't realised at first that dating a single mother meant that he would have five people to keep happy rather than just one. But then there had been moments, like when they had walked around the town fair, when it seemed to be working. And then some guy had been thrown off a roof and it had all gone to hell.

He drummed his fingers on the car dashboard, then sent a gif of Harry Potter chasing Darth Vader around on a broomstick. He didn't really understand it, but he knew that Mary loved all fandoms and hopefully it would get him back in the good books.

Heart a little lighter, he drove to the pub opposite the police station where he had promised to meet Macleod for a quick dinner. The Inspector was already there, looking a little miserable with his on-the-job orange juice.

"Go to the bar and order us three fish and chips," Macleod said as soon as Walker arrived. "Suzie O'Connor is on her way too. I've drafted her in from Edinburgh. You've worked with her before, is that right?"

"Yes." Walker liked Suzie. When he had worked with her before she hadn't minded him muscling his way into the investigation. She had only just moved over to the Major Investigation Team and Walker was dying to pick her brains about how she had made the switch out of uniform.

"How is the CCTV going?" Walker asked as he sat down with a soft drink of his own.

"Needle in a haystack," Macleod grumbled. His teuchter accent was always stronger when he was annoyed. "I hate to think that we might miss something just because there's so much footage. And the lads are knackered from watching hours of the stuff. There's always a chance that a vital clue might slip through the net."

"No sign of either of the other two stonemasons on the video?"

"Not yet. And there's no suggestion that their cars or vans were anywhere near the Abbey. But they could have got there by bus or taxi. Besides, we've had forensics go over that scaffolding inch by inch. There's no other fingerprints or DNA except those of the three stonemasons."

Suzie O'Connor walked in just as the waiter delivered three steaming plates of fish and chips. It was a coppers' pub and they knew the sort of thing their clientele desired which was dimly lit rooms and massive portion sizes.

Walker grabbed Suzie a cola from the bar and came back to hear her update the DI.

"We've just had the phone records back and it's good and bad news," Suzie said, grabbing a fork.

"Please tell me the good is better than the bad," Macleod said.

"Depends how you look at it. Both Cameron and Finlayson were in the centre of town that day. Now, Cameron already told us that he'd gone in to see the fair with his wife and kid, but Finlayson lied to us. He said he never left home."

"Can we tell if they went into the Abbey?"

"Not from the phone records. Only that they were in the general area, but then so were twenty thousand other people."

Macleod grunted. "At least that gives us something to go back to Finlayson with. What about Paul Cameron though? I like his chances better with that history of violent assault."

"Again, we're rechecking the CCTV to see if we can catch him separate from his family, but the wife claims they were together the whole time."

Macleod put down his fork. "I thought CCTV was supposed to make things better for us. Oppressing the masses should be easier than this."

"We've got a dozen Constables on it now," Walker said. "We've got to find something soon."

"Don't bet your last chip on it," Macleod chuckled.

Suzie straightened her dark ponytail which was already perfectly smooth. She even looked like promotion material. Walker wondered if she would be up for mentoring him, and wished that he had had the time to iron his shirt collar that day.

"I think we need to take another look at the physical evidence," Suzie said. "We need to find a way to rule out, or rule in, either Cameron or Finlayson."

"What about the murder weapon?"

Suzie tilted her head to one side. "No prints. But I could get the guys at the lab to have another look, see if there might be anything else to connect it to one of our men."

"Worth a try. All right, we're all knackered here, let's head home for some kip and regroup tomorrow. With any luck, we'll get a confession out of Finlayson or Cameron." Macleod's face told them just how likely he thought that was.

They went their separate ways and as Walker was driving back home, a call came through on his radio.

"Have you clocked off yet?" Dispatch asked.

Walker checked his watch. "Still on for a few minutes. What is it?"

"Domestic disturbance at an address near your location. Reports of a weapon unconfirmed, possibly a blade. We've already sent one car but we need a second."

"Any other info?"

"Looks like a neighbours' dispute that has escalated."

"What's the address?" Walker asked, even though he already thought he might know.

"Lochwinnoch Drive."

"I'll attend. I was there a few days ago and I think I know the participants."

"Understood."

By the time Walker arrived at the familiar part of Lochwinnoch Drive, there was a police car and an ambulance in attendance. Walker swore under his breath. He had worried that this dispute wouldn't be as easily solved as the WWC had planned. At least he knew that Mary was safely at home. She had texted him a picture of her watching Buffy the Vampire Slayer in her Team Spike dressing gown just a few minutes before.

"Look it's the cavalry," Neil Michelson said as he arrived at the house. "I hope you've brought a chainsaw."

"What do you mean?"

"The suspect has only gone and glued himself to the fence."

"Of course he has," Walker said with a sigh. "That would just be the perfect thing to happen today. Dispatch said there was a blade involved."

"Aye. Mrs Mackenzie was threatening to chop his arms off at the wrists with her garden shears. We think she was joking about that. Anyway, it's your problem now. Macleod wants me to nip into all the local cafés. We still don't know where Guthrie went for lunch on the day he died. I'm thinking I might get a free poke of chips out of it if they like the look of my uniform."

"And I'm left with a bloke glued to a fence."

Neil gave him a double thumbs up, and a Fonz-style grin. "Looks like it."

It wasn't until he walked towards the other men in uniform that he realised he was in the neighbouring garden to the one he was in last time. That must mean that it was Mr Biggins's property. Walker wasn't much of a gardener. He had an orchid that Mary gave him once and he had managed to keep that alive for more than a month, but that was about it. From what he could tell, Mr Biggins liked things more wild than his neighbour did, with more bushes and trees and fewer of the tiny animal statues that gave him the creeps.

Worse than any creepy statue however was the sight of the man attached to the fence. Mr Biggins stood with his arms splayed to either side like he had been given the order to be searched. A Constable stood on either side of him, both with the expressions of boredom and displeasure that often accompanied such a police call-out.

"Are you all right, Mr Biggins?" Walker asked. Mr Biggins was not exactly young and the position must have been uncomfortable for him. The last thing the Sergeant needed was the man to keel over.

"Quite all right," Biggins said stiffly. "Just proving my point."

"We would rather you had done that in a more diplomatic way," Walker suggested. The other man said nothing. He looked more embarrassed than defiant.

Walker took one of the Constables to one side for a quick run-down of events. Constable Harrow had just joined them from Glasgow that month, and his face told Walker all he needed to know about the young man's feelings about small-town life.

"Mrs Mackenzie called us out half an hour ago. She was cutting back some bushes along the fence, and Mr Biggins took exception to it. He came over here to stop her and... well, you can see what happened."

"What made him use the glue?"

"God knows, but we can't shift him without hurting him. We've put a call out for paramedics, but as it's not an urgent case they might be a while."

"That's just great," Walker said.

"I know. And I haven't had any dinner yet."

Walker didn't think it kind to mention that he had been treated to a fish supper by the DI.

"Mr Biggins? You know that you're going to face a charge for this." Walker explained to the man when he walked back over to the fence.

"It's her that should face a charge. Touching my trees. My wife planted them before she died."

Walker might have felt sorry for him, were it not for the fact that he should have been catching a murderer, not standing in a shrubbery.

"I thought we agreed you would leave it to the solicitors."

"Ha, and look where that got me! Bloody lawyers. It's just like that OJ Simpson thing all over again."

Walker felt a smile tug at the corner of his mouth, but he managed to keep it at bay.

Harrow tapped him on the shoulder. "Can you have a word with Mrs Mackenzie? That's her staring out of the patio doors. We took her in to stop the shouting. Some of the language she was using made PC Gallows blush and he was brought up in Springburn."

"All right. Just don't go anywhere, Mr Biggins," Walker said, unable to resist.

"Ha bloody ha."

Chapter 15: Bernie

Bernie had just got back from a Pilates class when she received a text from Julia, Mrs Guthrie's cleaner. She had sent the names of the streets that she remembered seeing on Alexander Guthrie's laptop. They were all near the South of the town, an area the locals called the Braes. Bernie normally liked a puzzle, but this one seemed a bit of a dead end. The main feature of the Braes was that there was nothing there. Most of it was a nature reserve with a couple of roads running through it. A place people went to walk dogs, only the Guthries didn't own one. Bernie added it to the spreadsheet for the case anyway. Sometimes these things could be important at a later date, although unless she discovered that the Guthries had a passion for the outdoors…

Hang on, what if passion was the issue here? *Find out if the Guthrie's were into dogging*, Bernie wrote down in the case file, hoping that Mary would realise she didn't mean anything to do with friendly canines.

She drummed her fingers on the kitchen counter. The meeting with Paul Cameron had unsettled her more than she had let on to Mary. Much as she wanted to believe that Mrs Guthrie had killed her husband, Cameron could not be ignored as a suspect. Violent, short-tempered and not too bright. The perfect type to throw someone from the roof of a building. And yet Bernie had meant what she had said about the crime being premeditated. That didn't fit with Cameron's personality at all.

Was that where Annabel Guthrie came in? Could she have manipulated Cameron, got him to do the killing for her? Bernie felt this was much more likely. But how would she prove it? She couldn't access their messages and emails, not even Liz could do that. Maybe someone had seen them together? But who? Alyssa Cameron would be the obvious person to ask, but Bernie reckoned there was no way her husband would let her talk to the WWC.

A puzzle, but an enjoyable one to chew over while Bernie made herself a supper of a Buddha bowl with long-grain rice and smoked salmon. She was just about to tuck in when her phone rang.

Bernie was surprised to see it was Alice who was calling. They were managing their new-found truce by avoiding one another as much as possible. So far they had been communicating largely by emails and texts.

"Hello?"

"You're not hearing this from me, but there's a big fuss going down with some of your former clients?"

"Oh?" Bernie put down her cup of tea. "Who?"

"The neighbour dispute. Biggins and Mackenzie. We've just had a call-out for a couple of cars to attend."

Bernie tutted under her breath. "I'll get right over there. Honestly, some people just won't take a telling. It's just like that time in the care home when we had Rabbi Jones and Nigel Royston from the cricket club getting into fisticuffs over who had the best view of the carpark.

"I hope you can sort it out before it gets to physical violence."

"We'll see," Bernie said, thinking that a quick slap for both of them might make them see sense. "Thanks for telling me."

"I'm just finishing my shift so I figured no one would connect me to you."

"What are you up to now? I could do with some help on the Abbey case."

Alice coughed. "Actually, I've got a date."

"Male? Female? Vegetable, animal or mineral?" Bernie asked. Alice's dating preferences were a bit of a family mystery.

"Ugh, don't try and be woke, Auntie, it doesn't suit you." Alice clicked off the call.

Bernie put her dinner into the fridge for later and made her way out to her car. She put the local news station on and made her way out of the drive. She used to listen to music in the car – classic rock, mostly – but now that she was in the business of solving crime she stuck to the local news channels. You never knew when you might hear something interesting. She had been trying to get Alice to nick her a police scanner, but apparently that sort of thing was frowned upon.

A few minutes later she pulled up at her destination. What concerned Bernie most when she arrived at Lochwinnoch Drive to see three police cars and an ambulance was how to charge for the hours when the case was already supposed to be finished. Normally, she would have those sorts of things laid out for the clients, but this was supposed to be a simple planning dispute. Really, Bernie thought, she should have known better. In the care home the worst arguments always occurred over the pettiest issues, like when Mrs Gammage's scarf had disappeared into Mrs Stevenson's wardrobe. A simple error by the cleaners had seen Mrs Stevenson take a Zimmer frame hit to the knees and Mrs Gammage had had a crown knocked out.

The two residents of Lochwinnoch Drive were a little younger than most of the care home residents, but the same principle applied. Put two people in close proximity and they will find something to fall out about. It was just like kids, only these two were a bit too old to clunk their heads together and tell them to share their toys.

When Bernie let herself in the gate, she hadn't quite been prepared for what she was about to see. There were several uniformed police officers milling around and most seemed to be clustered at the fence. It took a few seconds before Bernie understood that Mr Biggins seemed to be attached to it.

"He's glued himself to the fence, the stupid sod," a male Constable said into his radio as Bernie walked past him. She walked more quickly towards the fence, eager to see if it was true.

"You can't just come in here," a young Constable said, blocking her path. He had hair that was long on top, almost curly, and Bernie was sure that wasn't regulation length. Now was probably not the time to tell him that, given that he was already reaching for his phone.

"I'm working for Mr Biggins in a legal capacity," Bernie said quickly. "I wondered if I could be of some assistance."

The Constable relaxed a little. "I'm not sure what you can do right now. The paramedics have arrived, but they don't have the right tools or something, so they're going to send for the fire brigade. If you ask me, Mr Biggins is feeling rather foolish."

"What was your name?"

"Constable Harrow."

"Well, Harrow, I'm afraid to tell you that it is the most foolish among us who never quite cotton on to the fact that they have made themselves fools."

"Is that a quote from someone?"

"Yes. Me." Bernie spotted a familiar figure. Walker was in the kitchen of the house, chatting with Mrs Mackenzie. She turned around so that he could only see her back. She wasn't quite ready to be recognised yet.

"Take me to my client, please," Bernie said.

For a moment, she thought the Constable might say no. Then he gave the immortal shrug that said, let's make you someone else's problem, and let her follow him over to the fence.

"Hello Mr Biggins, I didn't think you'd be out here playing silly buggers with us," Bernie said, giving the old man's ear a tweak.

"Ouch! Get your hands off me, woman."

"Don't you woman me. What on earth was the point in paying us to solve this problem for you if you were going to do something stupid like this?"

"You didn't solve anything, did you? And now she can cut down my wife's trees whenever she likes."

Bernie folded her arms. If there was one thing she couldn't stand, it was sentimentality. "Your wife is not those bloody trees you silly man. What do you think she would say if she could see you like this?"

Mr Biggins said nothing, but his head dropped low.

Bernie was about to dispense some more wisdom when she sensed a commotion behind her.

"What the hell are you doing here?" Sergeant Walker's face was set in a most unattractive expression.

"I'm here to help, of course. What else?"

"I have often wondered. How did you get in here?"

"He let me in," Bernie said, jerking her thumb at the Constable.

"She said she was his lawyer," Constable Harrow said.

"No, I didn't. I said I was working with him in a legal capacity, which is true. I'm part of a private investigative firm that was looking into the issue of the contested boundaries."

Harrow's neck was turning red. "Sorry," he mumbled.

Walker shrugged. "It's okay. Mrs Paterson is known to the police. For a variety of reasons."

"All good I hope," she said, giving the man a wink.

"Not really," Walker muttered, but she pretended not to hear him. "Look, you're not needed here. We have the fire brigade on their way to release Mr Biggins. Mrs Mackenzie is quite happy complaining to Constable Harrow about the local bin collections, which she seems to think are his responsibility. So if you wouldn't mind clearing out, it would be very –"

Bernie's phone rang. "Sorry, I need to take this."

She turned away so that the police officer with the outraged face was looking at her back.

"Bernie Paterson, Wronged Women's Co-operative, how can I help you?"

A whispery voice spoke. "Hello dear. I heard from my friend in the care home that you were looking for someone that knew about the Abbey."

"Yes?"

"And I do," the voice said.

"Do what?"

"I know about the Abbey. My name is Mr Smail."

Smail. Where had she heard that name? Ah yes, Mary had mentioned him.

"You were at the Abbey when Alexander Guthrie was killed."

"Ah yes, poor man."

"Then I need to speak to you. I've got a bit of business to conclude here. Give me ten minutes…" Bernie glanced over at the fence. "Maybe fifteen minutes and I'll come and ask you some questions."

"Oh. I'm not at work right now."

"Even better. Give me your address and I'll come and see you at home."

"Oh. All right, tomorrow morning?"

"Perfect."

With some reluctance, Mr Smail gave her his home address and Bernie ended the call.

The angry-looking Sergeant Walker had wandered back to the fence, where Mr Biggins still seemed to be causing trouble. The group of officers looked a little confused as to what to do. They ought to try and shift at the care home, Bernie thought as she made her way over to them. That would give them an insight into just how difficult some men became when they hit their later years.

Bernie glanced at her watch. It was time to be going. She liked to get a run in before it got too dark, and her steps were already low for the day. She walked back to the fence.

"Look here, Mr Biggins, I can't help but feel that this whole thing has got a bit out of hand."

The old man's head still drooped. "I just wanted her to see how much trouble she was causing me. I saw the glue from where I'd been fixing the decking and... I just did it without thinking. And now they're going to arrest me, aren't they?"

"I should think so," Bernie said brightly. "That man, Sergeant Walker," she pointed to the other end of the garden where Walker was in discussions with the paramedics. "He reckons you're a total plonker."

"He said that?"

"Oh yes. And some other things. Something about old men who never paid their taxes."

Mr Biggins' back straightened. "Never paid my... I worked until I was sixty-five. What an arrogant young prick."

"My feelings exactly. You could tell him yourself, of course, were it not for your current situation."

Mr Biggins sighed. "What a mess. I thought it would be fun. I saw Extinction Rebellion do it once at Kew Gardens."

"Extinction Rebellion?" Bernie couldn't quite see the connection, but who was she to judge the man's passion? Oh all right, she was judging it like billy-oh, but still, there was something almost noble about the whole thing. Almost.

"Seems to me that if you wanted to, I could get you off that fence in a jiffy and you could give Sergeant Walker a piece of your mind."

"That does sound appealing. But I am rather stuck here you know."

"Nail polish remover," Bernie said with certainty. "I bet that Mrs Mackenzie has a big old bottle of it somewhere. That'll dissolve the glue."

"Are you sure?"

"My son used to do model making. Those little planes that you stick together. The number of times he would get a propeller shaft stuck to his thumb… Yeah, I'm sure."

"All right then. You get the stuff. I'll wait here"

It only took five minutes with Mrs Mackenzie to find out she had an industrial sized bottle of nail polish remover in her bedroom.

"But why should I help that silly little man?" she said.

"Oh, do you know, I think this was all an attempt to impress you," Bernie said, trying everything she could think of to resolve things before it got dark. "He's a man of action, that Mr Biggins, you've got to give him that."

Mrs Mackenzie looked more bewildered than impressed by this take on the situation, but she did agree to hand over the nail polish remover.

Rather than wait for the paramedics – who would probably want to do all sorts of boring checks – Bernie took the bottle straight over to the fence and pored the whole lot over Mr Biggins' hands.

"Bloody hell, that stinks," the old man said, and he wasn't wrong.

"Try moving your hands," Bernie said after a few seconds.

"What the hell is going on?" Walker asked.

"I'm saving the day, of course," Bernie said, just as Mr Biggins wrenched his hands from the fence.

Bernie couldn't help but grin. She might even make it back in time to do some more digging on Mrs Guthrie. And then she could work out exactly how much to bill Mrs Mackenzie and Mr Biggins for the happy resolution to all their problems.

That was the moment that Mr Biggins pulled his hand back and punched Sergeant Walker on the chin.

Chapter 16: Liz

The summer sun had begun to set by the time Liz arrived at the Abbey. Invergryff wasn't like Glasgow or Edinburgh. By the time that people had gone home from work on a weekday, the town centre was silent. If it hadn't been the town she had grown up in, Liz might have found it creepy.

The heavy breathing was a little scary, she thought as she made her way to the doors of the Abbey. Lucky it was her own, the weight of the baby making her wheeze as she climbed up the steps.

Liz wasn't entirely sure what the religious status of the Abbey was. It had a Reverend, and services several times a week, but also a tea room and gift shop. Her mother, Grace, liked the sort of church where people dressed up and sang loudly and enthusiastically, and that didn't seem to be the deal here.

Still, she wasn't there to worship so she waited outside on the steps until the service finished. Really, she shouldn't have been there at all. Bernie had only asked her to research the finances of the main suspects, and she could have done that from home. But she needed something to take her mind off her upcoming labour and what better than a murder investigation?

After a short wait, a couple of dozen people came out of the Abbey, chattering amongst themselves. When the last one left, Liz caught the door and slipped inside.

The Abbey when it was empty was definitely veering into the

creepy category. Liz was grateful to see that the Reverend was still there and she hadn't missed him.

Reverend McDade had that Scottish skin that is so pale it was almost devoid of colour. He was in his fifties or early sixties with watery blue eyes that widened when he saw the person approaching him. It was amazing how unsettling some men found a heavily pregnant woman. The Reverend looked at her like she was one of those lone tigers that was roaming a bit too close to civilisation.

"Hello," he said. "I'm afraid you missed the service. And choir practice isn't on tonight."

"My name is Liz Okoro," she said, walking over to him. "I'm not here for the service."

"Ah, then do you sing?"

"Only when no one's listening," Liz replied. "I was wondering if you might have a minute to spare."

"I have several slots available tomorrow, if you would like to –"

"I'm afraid I already have an important appointment booked for tomorrow," Liz said, pointing at her stomach. If anything, the Reverend turned even paler.

"All right, I can spare a few moments. You're a parishioner here?"

"Not exactly," Liz said. "Or rather, that's not why I'm here. I've been sent along by the Committee for Parish Accounts."

The Reverend put his hand to his mouth as if she had said that she had climbed out of the depths of hell itself. Liz was glad she had done some intensive internet searching to work out which body kept an eye on High Church finances.

"The Committee? It's a funny time of night for them to get in touch."

"I think they believed that it was an urgent matter."

Liz found her eyes drawn to the corner of the Abbey where the scaffolding still stood. Had this worried-looking man had something to do with the man who had so recently fallen from it?

"Why don't you come into my office? We can talk there."

Compared to the glamour of the vaulted main hall, the Reverend's office was a standard concrete box stuck onto one side of the Abbey. It had a large Victorian-style desk in the centre, a wardrobe and many shelves of books and paperwork.

"I can't offer you a drink I'm afraid. The kettle's broken."

There was something off about the Reverend. He seemed nervous in a way that Liz wouldn't have expected from someone that spent all his life talking to people. Did he know something about the death of Alexander Guthrie? His alibi was watertight, according to Bernie, so it hadn't been him hiding up in the scaffolding.

"You said you were from the Committee," the Reverend prompted.

"Yes. The thing is, part of my job is to look into the accounts."

"There's nothing wrong with our accounts. We're audited along with every other working Church."

"That's right, there was nothing wrong with the Abbey's accounts." Liz paused for a second to let this sink in. "But I did notice something a bit strange about your personal accounts."

"Oh?"

"You seem to be in a fair bit of debt. And I just wondered what that was all about?"

For a moment, Liz thought the Reverend was going to confess everything to her. Then he tightened his jaw. "I'm not sure you're really from the committee at all. Do you have some sort of identification?"

Liz was almost impressed that the Reverend had found a backbone, albeit at an inconvenient moment for her own investigations.

"Why don't you just tell me what's going on," she said, trying a different tactic. "I don't think you killed anyone, but you need to come clean about the money."

"Killed anyone? Of course I haven't killed anyone."

"But can't you see that it looks suspicious? Alexander Guthrie is killed, and when we take a look at your accounts they don't quite add up. What are the police going to think?"

The Reverend put his hand to his mouth like he was going to be sick. "They wouldn't think that. There's no connection to that poor man."

"Then what –"

"Enough! I wish to be alone with my God."

The baby inside her twirled around and poked at her ribs. It was time to go.

"You can call me any time," Liz said, handing over her card. It was one of a set that Bernie had ordered for the members of the WWC. Co-operative was spelt wrong, but Liz hadn't had the heart to tell her.

The Reverend took the card like it was a handshake from the devil. That is to say, reluctantly. After that, there was nothing for Liz to do but leave the Abbey.

Before she was back at her car, her phone rang. For a moment she thought it might be the Reverend, his conscience working quickly. That was until a female voice spoke.

"It's Abbi. Abbi Musa."

For a moment, the pregnancy brain-fog meant that Liz couldn't think who that was, but then she remembered. Abbi was her mother's friend who stayed on Lochwinnoch Drive. Liz had asked her mother to give the woman a call and ask her to get in touch.

"Hi Abbi, thanks for phoning. Did my mum tell you what this was about?"

"Yes. You want to know about those stupid white people that are always fighting. Well, today they even had an ambulance up there. I thought maybe one of them had had a heart attack, but the ambulance went away with nobody in it."

"Ah, I think I know why." Liz had already had a series of cryptic messages from Bernie concerning the day's events that had unfolded on Lochwinnoch Drive. "Thank you for letting me know, but we've managed to resolve that case now."

"You don't need me anymore?"

"Not at the moment," Liz said, her mind already on what she needed to get ready for the hospital.

"I suppose you don't want to know about the dead man, either?"

"You mean Mr Biggins? He's fine I think, maybe some sore fingers for a few days, but..."

"Not him. The man that died at the Abbey."

Liz paused in her stride. "You know something about Alexander Guthrie?"

Just at that moment, the line began to crackle.

"So that's what I think," Abbie said, coming back on the line.

"Tell me what you said!" Liz shouted.

"Are you all right?"

"Yes. I mean, no. Your phone cut out and if this was a third-rate TV drama I would never find out what you knew about Alexander Guthrie! Now please tell me."

"All right," Abbi said in the tone of voice you would use with a rabid dog who was looking intently at your leg. "It's just a dodgy line. Your mother did say you were finding this pregnancy tough."

"She did? What exactly did she – No. Tell me about Guthrie."

"I used to work with his wife. In the social work department. She got fired."

"I didn't know that."

"It was a big drama. She worked with some vulnerable people and money went missing from their accounts. Nothing big, but all when Mrs Guthrie was working there. The money was all put back later, so they didn't report her or anything, but it got her the sack."

"Wow." Maybe Bernie was right and Mrs Guthrie did have a secret to hide.

"The funny thing is, Mr Guthrie called up a couple of weeks ago to speak to his wife. He had no idea that she had been fired. I don't think he was very happy about it."

"Now that is interesting. Thanks Abbi."

"You're welcome. Now maybe you should get some rest?"

"Of course," Liz said. Just as soon as I solve a murder and have a baby, she thought. Hopefully in that order.

Chapter 17: Mary

Mary knew something bad had happened. It didn't take a genius to work it out, to be fair. Walker had turned up at her house with an ice pack on his jaw and a furious expression on his face.

"Bernie Paterson!" He huffed as he walked in through Mary's front door.

"Oh god, she didn't hit you, did she?"

"Might as well have." Walker sat down on the sofa. This was a mistake as he was immediately surrounded by small children.

"What happened to your face?"

"Was it a crimininiminal?"

"Can I poke it?"

"Off to your rooms," Mary said, tugging the kids off the unlucky man. "If you stay up there and keep quiet for half an hour you can watch Dirty Dancing before bed."

Happy to accept the bribe the kids ran upstairs, leaving them alone.

"Is that film age appropriate?" Walker asked, settling into a more comfortable position on the sofa.

"They only get to see the dancing bits. I fast forward the sex."

Mary sat down beside him. "Your jaw doesn't look too bad," she said, placing her hand on his cheek.

"Oh, I know that. I'm just trying to keep the swelling down so that the lads at the station don't take the Mickey any more than they have already."

Walker explained exactly what had happened.

"I can't believe Mr Biggins had it in him," Mary said. "But I don't see how you can blame Bernie."

"Apparently she was telling him something about losing face to the big bad police officer. So then when I told him not to play any more silly beggars he 'saw red'. He was very apologetic afterwards."

"Are you going to press charges?"

"He'll get a caution. And a right good telling-off. As for Bernie Paterson, I'm working my way through the police handbook and I'm sure I'm going to find something to charge her with."

"I'm sure she didn't mean to do anything."

Walker gave raised an eyebrow.

"Well, maybe eighty per cent sure."

"She's decided to take the Abbey case on I see," he said.

Mary looked down at the floor. There was a raisin flattened into the carpet. "We both have. I mean, I was there when it happened."

"I remember."

She waited for him to get to the point. One of the things that she liked about her boyfriend was that he didn't waste his words, but it meant that at that moment Mary felt like she was in court awaiting a verdict.

"Macleod isn't too happy about the WWC being involved."

"Because we've solved a case for him before?" Mary couldn't help but smile. "Maybe he's scared of the competition."

"I don't think he's petty like that. He just wants things done right."

"And we won't do it right?"

Walker breathed out a long sigh. "Why does this feel like a fight that neither of us can win?"

Mary leaned back against his arm. "You're right about that."

"So can we just agree to put it to one side for the moment?"

Was it just putting off an inevitable fallout? Possibly, but Mary was happy enough to go along with it while she was cuddled into his broad chest, her eyes half-closed already.

"You know that Bernie thinks Mrs Guthrie killed her husband," she said.

"Really? We've not found any evidence linking her to the scene. And I can't see her climbing up that scaffolding without anyone noticing."

"I know. But the thing is, Bernie went to school with her. She was a mean kid, used to bully Bernie back in the day."

"She bullied Bernie? Wow. She must be a hard case."

Mary shook her head. "You don't understand. Our Bernie is like... Bernie 2.0. When she was at school she was the chubby girl that everyone picked on."

"And then she lost weight and got tough?"

"Or she got tough and lost weight. I'm not too sure, you would have to ask Liz about it. But what I'm saying is, this Guthrie woman, she's basically part of Bernie's villain origin story."

"Huh. And won't Bernie be mad that you're telling me this?"

Why was she telling Walker? It had to be something to do with the creased up feeling in her stomach she got every time Bernie talked about the dead man's wife.

"I think she might be making a mistake," Mary said finally. "She's always so controlled with her emotions, you know? And this time I think they might be getting the better of her. I'm telling you because I want you to look out for her. She's not thinking clearly at the moment."

"Isn't that more of a reason for you to drop the case?" Walker suggested.

Mary rolled her eyes. "Hardly. It means that I need to be right beside her, making sure she does the right thing. If Bernie Paterson is going to make a mistake for the first time in her life, she's going to need a friend to pick up the pieces for her."

"Do you ever think…? No, it doesn't matter."

"What?"

Walker bit his bottom lip. "I just wonder if Bernie would do the same for you."

"Oh yes, she would. She's a nightmare, but she's a loyal nightmare. Like if you had an angry, rage-driven Labrador."

A small tousled head poked around the corner of the living room door. "Can we play Mario Kart?"

"Not just now."

Walker had sat up a little straighter. "They have Mario Kart?"

"Yeah. It's not the same as when we were young though. It's a lot harder."

"I bet I could give it a good shot. I used to be unbeatable as Princess Peach."

An hour later Walker and the kids were deep into a video game tournament. Mary hummed to herself as she watched them. Walker hadn't even mentioned his chin the whole time.

"Can Walker stay all night?" Peter asked as he pummelled the police officer with an array of comedic missiles.

Mary shrugged. "I guess so," she said. At that moment her boyfriend drove straight off the track.

Chapter 18: Walker

On Wednesday morning, Walker woke up with a pain in his jaw but the heady sensation of being officially allowed to stay over at his girlfriend's house. Of course, that should be a given for a couple in their thirties, but the children had always complicated things somewhat. Neither Mary nor he had wanted to let them down by moving things along too quickly. Something had changed, however, and Walker wasn't sure if it was solely that someone had punched him in the face.

He got dressed while Mary was still fast asleep and only woke her to let her know he was heading off to work. By the time he had dry swallowed some painkillers and grabbed a bacon roll from the snack van near the station, he was starting to feel on top of the world.

"You look like crap," Suzie O'Connor said as he walked into the office.

"Thanks for that."

"I heard you got a little something on your chin," she said with a wink.

"I take it everyone knows?"

"Are you kidding? You get punched by an octogenarian in his rose bushes, you think that isn't the most exciting thing we've heard all month?"

"Just great. And he wasn't much past seventy."

O'Connor walked away still laughing. In truth, Walker wasn't too bothered. It wasn't the first time that he'd given his colleagues a laugh and it wouldn't be the last. His relationship success was enough to keep his good mood in place. The only thing that was bothering him that morning was the lack of progress on the Guthrie murder.

"How is that CCTV coming along?" Walker asked.

"Still nothing definitive on our two main suspects," Constable Harrow said. "But we found out where he went for lunch. We've got footage of him going into a local restaurant, Petra, then coming out again an hour or so later."

"And do we know who he was meeting?"

"We're checking the cameras. Sergeant Michelson has gone to speak to the people at the restaurant too, find out if they saw who he was with."

"Good work," Walker said, pleased that there had been some progress. He knew that Neil would enjoy visiting the restaurant and just hoped he would bring back enough food for all of them.

DI Macleod came into the room, banging the door shut as he did so.

"We've got a problem," he said. "Paul Cameron has gone AWOL. A couple of uniforms went to pick him up for questioning this morning and he's nowhere to be found. The wife claims he went to work but he's not there either."

"You think he's done a runner?"

"Most likely. I want his number-plates flagged up on all the systems, and put his description out to the press. He's got form for violence so we can't afford to be slow on this one. I've already cleared it with the Superintendent. Sergeant O'Connor's in charge of this one."

Suzie nodded and started to organise the Constables. Walker went over to help them but Macleod caught him by the arm.

"Can I have a word, Sergeant?"

Walker followed the DI into his office, assuming that he was about to get a telling-off about the Biggins debacle, but Macleod had something else on his mind.

"Alyssa Cameron had a couple of visitors yesterday."

Walker's heart sank. "Did she?"

"I wonder if you can guess who they were."

The Sergeant said nothing. He had found it was always the best course with superior officers when you were in big trouble.

Macleod leaned back in his chair and glared at him. "I have managed to keep your name out of it with the Superintendent, but if we don't find Cameron quickly then the whole thing with your girlfriend and her friends is going to come out. And it's not going to go well for you."

"It is their job, sir," Walker said. "Even if I don't like it much.

And they do manage to get results, often where we wouldn't be able to."

"And the reason they can do that is that they don't follow the law. And that's what makes them so dangerous. At any moment they could put a conviction at risk. Do they realise that?"

Walker felt sweat gather on his forehead. "I think they just want to help."

Macleod looked out of the window. "You told me once that you wanted to be a detective. And I think you have the brains for it. But do you realise the problem you'll have if you do get a position with CID?"

"What?"

"You'll more than likely have to move. And it won't be a three-month thing like when you did your Sergeant's training in Edinburgh. You're looking at a two-year posting."

Walker had realised that, but the implication hadn't really set in before. Now that Macleod was spelling it out for him, it was leaving a twisted feeling in his stomach.

"This thing with the divorced woman is pretty serious, then?"

"As serious as it gets, sir."

Macleod ran his hand over his stubbly chin. "Maybe you need to have a conversation with her. She's not going to move the kids out of school to relocate with you."

"No. And I wouldn't ask her to."

"Well, you know your own mind I'm sure," Macleod said, standing up to indicate that the awkward conversation was over. "Just try and keep your relationship out of this investigation, okay?"

"Yes sir."

Suzie O'Connor was waiting for them when they came out. She gave Walker a quizzical look. News of a bollocking always got around the station quickly, but he was in no mind to discuss it with her.

"Still no sign of Cameron. I was at his house earlier. The wife was in a bit of a state. I've brought her in for an interview and I've put an alert out for him with the press, both the nationals and the locals. I've got them to emphasise that he shouldn't be approached. Hopefully, someone will turn him in."

Macleod chewed his thumbnail. "He's a probable danger to the public. And I'd say this puts him in prime position for the killing of Alexander Guthrie. Walker, you go back over everything we've got on him. Find me a reason for him to kill Guthrie so that when we get hold of the bastard we'll be able to present him to the Procurator Fiscal wrapped up in a bow."

"Yes sir," Walker said, eager to get back to some proper police work. Maybe if he worked hard enough he would forget what Macleod had said about his future. And just what the hell it might turn out to be.

Chapter 19: Bernie

As far as Bernie was concerned, the previous day had gone well. Yes, Sergeant Walker hadn't been best pleased when Mr Biggins had thumped him one, but it had stopped the two neighbours arguing for a few minutes. As Mrs Mackenzie had applied a bag of frozen peas to the police officer's face, Mr Biggins had made him a cup of tea and for a few moments they were an unlikely partnership. That was worth a crack on the jaw in Bernie's book.

Something that was irritating Bernie was their lack of progress in the Alexander Guthrie case. She had turned on the news that morning to see a grainy mugshot of Paul Cameron on the morning news. She had texted Mary to complain that Walker hadn't given them advance notice that the man had done a runner, but her friend hadn't replied.

Despite the actions of Mr Cameron, Bernie still reckoned that Annabel Guthrie was the killer. She would find the evidence she needed. It was just a matter of time. Until then she would investigate all the other possible suspects. She knew that the other members of the WWC were not convinced of Annabel Guthrie's guilt, so she was going to do her best to persuade them. And the best way to do that was cold hard facts.

First of all, she had to meet with Mr Smail from the Abbey. Bernie knew he had witnessed the fall and she just had to hope that he had noticed something more interesting than Mary Plunkett, who had clearly been too busy making moon eyes at her boyfriend to spot any clues.

From the description of Mr Smail that Mary had given her – tiny, frail, someone you would imagine tending a greenhouse – Bernie had assumed that the man would live in an old cottage somewhere. So she was surprised to find that his address was a rather smart block of flats in the town centre not more than half a mile from the Abbey itself.

"Easy to maintain, you see," Smail explained as he showed her into the living room. The only outside space was a small balcony that overlooked a busy road and didn't appear to be used. "The Abbey takes up so much of my time."

"I can imagine," Bernie said, even though she couldn't. It occurred to her that she wasn't entirely sure what it was that the man did.

"The Reverend relies on me, you see. He often has duties that take him out of the parish."

Bernie had never been a fan of small talk. "Like the day when the man was killed. He wasn't there, was he?"

"Ah, sadly not. I'm sure it would have been a comfort to all of us who were there if he had been around to say some kind words. Still, I hope that I managed to help in my own small way."

The man gave a sort of smug little smile. Bernie decided that she didn't like him one bit. He had that sort of beta personality that begged for constant reassurance.

"I hope you don't mind an instant coffee," Smail said with an apologetic smile. "I used to have one of those machines in my old place, but I didn't bother bringing it here."

Bernie noticed that despite the absence of furniture there was a layer of dust over everything and cobwebs on the windows. She tutted inside her head. What was the point in all this modernist perfection if you didn't even do your chores? No wonder he wasn't married. No woman would put up with it.

"Now I would like to know why you gave me a call, Mr Smail," Bernie said, taking a sip of what turned out to be an exceptionally terrible cup of coffee.

"Ah. Well, I had heard that you were a member of a private agency that specialised in..." he waved his hands around looking for the right word. "Detection?"

"I am the owner and director of the agency, yes," Bernie said. "What was it that you wanted to bring to our attention?"

"It's rather the opposite, in fact. I would like some things to *not* be brought to your attention. Things that have no relevance whatsoever to the unfortunate death of Mr Guthrie."

Bernie didn't have much patience for this sort of chatter. "What exactly do you mean?"

"There has been some talk doing the rounds of our staff members that your people have been seeking out... Well, what might be nothing more than petty gossip about members of our community. That you have been digging around trying to find something and come up with a whole lot of irrelevant tittle-tattle."

"Spit it out, man," Bernie said.

Mr Smail blinked. "I'm sorry if my caution offends you, but you must understand that we have reputations to protect."

Bernie leaned forward. "It seems to me that the only person who has a reputation in need of protecting is the Reverend. That is who you are worried about, am I correct?"

Smail squirmed in his chair. "I never said so."

"No. Mr Smail, I completely understand that you are loyal to the Reverend, but do you know where loyalty gets you?"

"Where?"

"In a police cell charged with obstruction."

"But... you're not police?" Mr Smail brought out an old-fashioned handkerchief and wiped his brow.

"No, but I have a duty to pass information pertinent to a crime on to them. The same duty that you have."

"But there isn't... that's what I'm trying to tell you. The Reverend has nothing to do with this dreadful murder."

"And you can prove that, can you?"

"Not as such, no. But Reverend McDade is not a bad man."

"Is he a good one?"

Smail twisted the handkerchief between his fingers. "He is human, as we all are."

"Is it a woman?"

Bingo! Smail sprung back in his chair like she had shot him.

"But the Reverend is Church of Scotland, isn't he? So it can't be a problem unless she's married."

Smail pressed his lips together.

"It wouldn't be Annabel Guthrie, by any chance?"

For a moment, Bernie thought she had him. Then Smail let out a gasp of horror.

"Guthrie's wife? You think he murdered the man because he was having an affair with his wife? It must be a dark life you live indeed to imagine such things."

Disappointed, Bernie downed the last of the awful coffee. "A bog standard affair with someone else then. And that's what you're protecting him from? The scandal?"

Smail shrugged. "Perhaps."

Bernie let herself out. Mr Smail probably thought he had persuaded her to eliminate the Reverend from the list of suspects, but Bernie had seen a lot more of life than the Abbey manager. If the Reverend was afraid of a scandal, then that might be just the motivation he needed to push someone off a scaffold. She climbed into her car and drove home in a state of irritation. Mrs Guthrie was still in the clear and if anything she had added another suspect to the list. It was about time to start narrowing them down.

Chapter 20: Liz

"Can I get you anything?" Dave asked for the millionth time that day. Liz merely shook her head, not looking up from the laptop. Bernie had just updated the case file with some information from Smail. The Reverend was having an affair with someone. If Liz could dig a little deeper into his financial records she might just be able to find out who.

"Maybe we should have a wee chat about the hospital?" Dave asked.

"It's all in hand," Liz replied.

"Ah. Right. Perhaps we could –"

Liz raised her eyes from the screen. "I love you, but unless you have something important to say about the Alexander Guthrie case, I really could do without the interruptions. And if you're going to mention anything to do with the fact that someone is going to be cutting me open in a few hours, I'd rather not hear it."

"Well, it's lucky that it's the former then."

Liz frowned. "What?"

"Guthrie. I do have something to tell you about him. If you shut that laptop down and come over here I'll give you a foot rub and tell you exactly what I mean."

She grunted assent and made her way over to the sofa where

she sat at the other end to her husband. She lifted her legs up and let Dave massage the balls of her aching feet. She had to admit it did feel pretty good.

"That feels amazing," she said. "I'm sorry I'm being such a bitch."

"I hadn't noticed."

"Liar. And don't say I'm allowed either."

Dave dug his fingers into her cramped muscles. Liz let out a little moan. "Don't stop, please."

"All right. Do you still want to hear about Guthrie?"

"I guess so," she said. Suddenly the case didn't seem quite so important.

"I had to look up my records to work out how I knew him. He had been coming to my clinic for a few years, just for the standard eye test, nothing out of the ordinary. I wouldn't even have remembered his name if it hadn't been for the injury."

"The injury?"

"Yeah, around a year ago he had an eye injury at work. It's pretty common for people that work on building sites to get stuff in their eyes. He had been treated at the hospital at the time and this was just a follow-up appointment."

"Do you know how it happened?"

"He got debris in his eyes. He was pretty worried about it, but we didn't find any significant vision loss."

"It can't have been at the Abbey," Liz said thoughtfully. "He wasn't working there then. I wonder what job that was on. Maybe it was one of those 'have you had an accident at work' insurance jobs and it got nasty?"

"I don't think so. He admitted he was at fault. He should have used protective goggles, of course. But he said that he'd been asked to do a homer for someone and hadn't put them on. He was pretty sheepish about it."

"He wasn't angry or threatening to sue or anything?" Liz asked hoping there might be a motive for someone to commit murder lurking in the story.

"I don't think so. He seemed fairly accepting of the whole thing. He did say a few things that were weird enough for me to remember the appointment though."

"What were they?"

"He said he had to hide the eye drops so that his wife wouldn't find them. I must have looked kind of shocked, because he just brushed it off as if it was nothing. But then later on when I had to sign off his insurance forms, he looked really relieved. I mean, that's not surprising. If I hadn't signed him off he wouldn't be able to work. But he made some comment about needing to keep the money coming in for 'the missus'. It was the two things together that struck me. I remember thinking I was glad that I married someone that was a bit more chilled out."

Liz laughed. "You wouldn't call me chilled out now, would you?"

Dave leaned over and stroked her bump. "Ah, but there are the extenuating circumstances."

"And it's temporary," Liz added.

Now it was Dave's turn to let out a chuckle. "Yeah, I'm sure you'll be chilled out when there's a newborn in the house waking every hour of the day."

Liz grimaced. "God, I'd forgotten what a nightmare the whole not sleeping thing is. Why did we ever decide to do this again?"

"Because we had Sean and he's the most awesome little human in the world," Dave reminded her. "Why wouldn't we want to have another one of them?"

Liz smiled. She knew he was right. It was so easy to focus on the whole labour thing and forget what the important bit was. The tiny human being who would soon be a part of their family.

"Do you want a cuppa?" Dave asked her.

"Yes please. Do you know, I think there was something seriously wrong in the Guthrie marriage. Abbi Musa told me that Mrs Guthrie had been fired and hadn't even told her husband. And now you're saying that Alexander didn't tell her about an eye injury. That can't be healthy, keeping those kinds of secrets."

"Other people's marriages are always a bit of a mystery," Dave said as he made his way through to the kitchen.

"Yeah, but they don't always end in murder. Damn it, I'm going to have to call Bernie and tell her she might have been right about Annabel Guthrie all along."

"She'll love that."

Liz sighed and reached for her phone. "I know."

Chapter 21: Mary

Mary loved the summer holidays. A lot of parents didn't, she knew. The lack of routine, having the children around twenty-four seven, the endless washing... Sure, those things could be a drag. But not having to get four kids up and dressed for school and nursery made up for it in spades. Plus, she enjoyed finding activities for them.

Today was a typical July day in Invergryff which had started with fog that had turned into the sort of constant drizzle that was just heavy enough to stop them from going to the park.

Mary decided to make biscuits. She only had gram flour from the day they had decided to make pakora and she had run out of sugar, but she used crushed-up breakfast cereal instead, and she was sure that it would be fine. She added a handful of raisins to make sure they would be healthy.

With some interesting smells coming from the oven, she set the kids to work on a board game. This was always something of a challenge. Lauren who was only four couldn't read, which made things like Monopoly tricky. They had decided to go for the classic 'Rings on my Fingers' and were now arguing about whose turn it was.

Ten minutes later the aim of the game had been forgotten but the whole bunch of them including the boys were enjoying being princesses with towels wrapped around their shoulders as capes and the plastic rings adorning every finger.

"Peter stole my sapphire!" A small voice wailed.

"Give it back, Peter," Mary said. She checked the biscuits. They had turned a rather lurid shade of yellow.

"Icing will cover it," she told herself and went to forage in the back of the cupboard for the bag of icing sugar and some food colouring.

The door rang just as she grabbed hold of the bag, meaning she whacked her head on the top of the cupboard in her hurry to get out.

"Ouch," Mary said, rubbing her head. She then realised that she had spilt a cloud of sugar down her top.

"Gran's here!" Vikki shouted.

That was just perfect, Mary thought, trying to brush the white powder from her front. Her mother was the sort of person who loved tidiness and never had a hair out of place. Of course she would choose this moment to visit.

"Hello children, are you all well today?" Nel said like something out of Mary Poppins. Mary's mum had grown up in Invergryff, but she always seemed like someone from another world.

"I can't stay long. I'm having my hair set at the new salon in town in an hour." Mary had always been too scared to ask how one set one's hair. Her own hair was half in a bun, half in a pleat that Vikki had put in when they had been watching cartoons that morning.

A timer dinged from the kitchen.

"That'll be the biscuits," Mary explained. "Come on through and I'll make you a cuppa."

Her mother followed her out of the living room of marauding children and into the relative sanctuary of the small galley kitchen.

"Are they meant to be that colour?"

"We're going to put icing on them," Mary said, her smile becoming one degree more brittle.

"This stuff? It's blue."

"Yes it is. Kids, time for biscuit decoration!" She took the biscuits and the icing through into the dining room and let the kids have at them. She just hoped that the blue wouldn't stain as it seemed to immediately cover every surface in the vicinity.

"How have you been?" Her mother asked.

"Busy. Thanks for taking the kids yesterday. This Abbey murder thing has been taking up all my time, especially as Liz is due any moment now."

"She must be anxious, what with her age and everything."

Mary blinked. "I mean, she's over forty, but she has had a baby before. I'm sure she'll be fine."

Just at that moment, Peter managed to flick some icing at Johnny. The younger boy ducked so that it spattered on the wall behind him.

"I'll get it," Mary said, trying her best to scrape the stuff off with a bit of kitchen towel. It didn't work.

"Why don't you all play outside for a bit," Mary said.

"It's raining," Vikki complained.

"Coats and wellies then."

Ten minutes later and there was some peace in the house once more. Nel helped Mary clean up the aftermath of the biscuits. Neither of them mentioned the fact that the kids hadn't eaten them.

"You had more room in your old kitchen," Nel said wistfully.

"I did." The five bedroom house with a luxury dining kitchen that she had shared with her ex-husband had indeed been larger than her current home in Invergryff. Pity the whole thing had been paid for by Matt's maxed-out credit cards.

"Stephanie lives in our old house now," Vikki called through from the patio doors. "She and Daddy do Body Pump together."

Nel's eyes widened.

"It's a fitness class," Mary said quickly. "Matt's girlfriend has got him going to the gym."

"Does she now," Nel said. "Well, I suppose she is rather younger than him. Maybe he feels he needs to keep himself in shape."

Mary smiled but said nothing. Trashing her ex-husband wasn't really her style. After all, it had been Mary that had left him in the end. And they had to parent the kids together whether they were nice to each other or not. Still, it was fun to let her mother comment on them just a tiny bit.

"How's the detecting going?" Nel asked.

"Slowly. You know, you would think the fact that I was there when it happened would give me some sort of advantage, but to be honest we're struggling with this case. There just doesn't seem to be a motive for the man's death."

"It couldn't have been an accident?"

"Not according to the post-mortem. Walker says that the evidence suggests that he was hit by one of his tools before he fell."

"How terrible."

"The two other stonemasons seem the most likely suspects. Sam Finlayson and Paul Cameron. And Cameron has just done a runner, so I guess he's top of the list. Bernie still thinks it must be the wife though."

"I'm sure it couldn't have been Sam Finlayson. He doesn't seem the murdering type."

"You know Finlayson?"

"A little. He used to play on the Bridge team. Him and his wife."

"His wife died, didn't she?"

"Yes. It was terribly sad."

"And people said that she was drunk behind the wheel, right?"

Nel pursed her lips. "I don't like to gossip."

Mary sighed. "Mum, gossip is how we solve half our cases. Please, if you know anything about the Finlaysons, it would be useful to tell me."

"Well, if you put it like that... I was surprised when people said about the drinking. Not just because it was such a sad story. I used to see Ginny Finlayson out sometimes. The week before she died she was at the British Legion for dinner. And she said she wasn't drinking. She was on a diet you see. Atkins, maybe, or that one where you don't eat after six in the evening. Your Auntie Pat has had rave results with intermittent fasting. She wore a bikini on her trip to Cyprus last month, can you imagine?"

Mary sifted through this information. "So you're saying that Ginny Finlayson wasn't drunk?"

"I think it's unlikely."

"I wonder where that rumour got started," Mary said, thinking out loud. "Maybe Walker might know if the post-mortem showed any alcohol in her system."

"It's still going well with that young policeman then?" Nel asked.

"He's only five years younger than me, mum," Mary said. "And they prefer 'police officers' these days."

"Do they?" Her mum grabbed a cloth and started wiping down the counters. "And he's good with the kids is he?"

"He loves them."

"Mmmn."

Her mum scrubbed at the tap. Mary could sense the unsaid words on her lips.

"What is it, mum?"

"You'll think I'm interfering."

Mary laughed. "You? Never!"

Nel looked younger when she smiled. "All right, perhaps I do give you my opinion a bit too freely. But I'm your mum and I worry about you. Just like you do with your own kids. And the thing is... look, I like Walker, but I know that you said you didn't want any more babies."

"I don't," Mary agreed. "When I was pregnant with Lauren it was a nightmare. My pelvis went and I could barely walk. And besides, I'm already outnumbered."

"Well then, I suppose my question is, what does Walker think about that?"

"What do you mean?"

"He's a young guy, Mary. Doesn't he want kids of his own?"

"He's never mentioned it."

Nel reached over and took her hand. "Do you mean you've never asked?"

Mary felt a little light-headed. Had they ever talked about whether or not he wanted kids? She didn't think so. But wasn't that the sort of thing that people did discuss? If they were in an adult relationship. So why hadn't it ever come up for her and Walker?

"I'm sorry to upset you, darling, but I don't want you going down the road where... well, where you might end up disappointed. After what happened with Matt, I just want you to be happy. You deserve to be happy."

"Thanks, mum," Mary whispered. She had the feeling that something dreadful had just happened, but how could it have done, in her own kitchen while the leftover biscuits dissolved in the sink? Her mum was probably wrong, Mary thought. Everything was going well with Walker. Or was it?

Chapter 22: Walker

Sergeant Walker thumped his desk. "Another dead end on Paul Cameron," he said when Neil Michelson looked at him. "No one from the Abbey has seen him today and he's meant to be on shift. They didn't get in touch with us because they didn't think it was important."

"The wife is still claiming she has no idea where he is," Neil said. "And Macleod's not going to be happy because we still can't find him on the CCTV on the day of the murder. The crowd around the Abbey is just too packed. He could be there and we would never see him."

"Have you tried around the portaloos?" Walker said, an idea occurring to him.

"No, but I could have a look. Why there in particular?"

"The Camerons have got a young kid. And I happen to know that any outing with children involves more trips to the loo than you would ever think possible."

"Good idea, mate, I'll give it a try."

Suzie O'Connor walked over to his desk. "I've got that second forensics report back on the murder weapon. There are still no full prints, but they think they might have a partial palm print. It wouldn't be enough for a definitive match, but it might be worth checking out once we get Cameron back in here."

"*If* we get him back in here," Walker said. "How are we doing on his known associates?"

Neil shrugged. "Apart from the wife, we haven't been able to find anyone. Since he moved up here he doesn't look to have socialised at all."

"Not even with Guthrie and Finlayson?"

"Not according to Sam Finlayson. I just spoke to him. He says that Cameron came in, did his work and went home. Finlayson also said that he thought Guthrie might not have liked Cameron much."

"Did he?" Walker didn't remember Finlayson mentioning that before.

"Yeah."

"Okay. Looks like we need to find who his contacts are from before he moved up here. Any family and friends that we can find."

Neil turned back to his computer. "Got it."

The Sergeant was about to go back into the files when his phone rang.

"Hello, it's DS Nicholls here from Tyneside returning a call from Sergeant Walker."

Walker always loved to hear the Newcastle accent. It reminded him of watching *Byker Grove* as a kid.

"Thanks for calling back. It's about a suspect in a murder case here. Paul Cameron."

"I saw on the news that he's done a runner."

"Aye. He was meant to come in for questioning but he's scarpered. I was wondering if you could tell us a wee bit more about him. You worked the assault case last year, is that right?"

"Yeah. And I can tell you that Paul Cameron is as nasty as they come. We only got him on the assault as one of the guys as we couldn't get CCTV for the aggravated assault, but we're certain that he did both, no matter what the jury said."

"That was his first run-in with the police?"

"Not quite. Three years ago there was a report of domestic assault. This was his previous girlfriend. Broke a couple of her ribs and pushed her down the stairs. But when it came to it she wouldn't testify against him."

"Can you give me her name?"

"Leanne Ipsom."

"Thanks."

The frustration was evident in Nicholls' voice. "He's a thug, Paul Cameron, that's the truth. I'm only surprised it's taken him this long to kill someone."

"What happened during the assault on the two men?"

"I've got the reports here. Cameron said one of them went for him, but according to the witnesses, it was Cameron that threw the first punch. And he wouldn't have stopped punching only there were witnesses. So he leaves off the first guy and goes around the corner. Finds some other poor sod and lays into him with a brick. The guy was lucky he got his arms up to protect his skull or he'd be dead. Broken arms, smashed up nose, the works. But not on CCTV, of course."

"Of course."

"Cameron managed to argue that it could have been one of the other lads milling about that night. There had been a few disturbances, it was a pretty rough area and there was always trouble in that pub. But most of the fights stopped when one person was down on the ground. Cameron only stopped when he had done real damage. As I said, a nasty piece of work."

"And he did time for it?"

"Eighteen months, down to twelve for the guilty plea, served six inside." It wasn't hard to work out what Nicholls thought about that one.

"Do you have any idea where he's gone? Any local lads from your neck of the woods that might give him a bed?"

"I've got my officers checking on the ground here for you. But he didn't seem like the sort of guy who had a lot of friends."

Walker breathed out a sigh. "Thanks for calling."

"Hope you get him," Nicholls said, clicking off the call.

It only took Walker a few minutes to find a number for a Miss

Leanne Ipsom in Newcastle. She was listed as working in a Beauty Salon in the city centre. Pretty soon he had her on the phone.

"Leanne Ipsom? It's Sergeant Owen Walker here from Invergryff Police Station."

"You're calling about Paul."

"That's right."

"I saw on the news that he'd done a runner. What are you after him for?"

"We want to talk to him in connection with the death of a man here."

"Right." The woman's voice was brittle, like she was having to control it to keep the conversation going.

"I don't suppose you have any idea where he might be?"

"Nowhere near here if he knows what's good for him."

"So you're not still in contact?"

"Not for years now. Not since I had to have my jaw rewired."

Walker grimaced. "Sorry to hear that."

"Don't be. It made me see Paul for what he really was. I knew that if I hung around long enough, he'd kill me."

She said it so matter-of-factly that it made a shiver trickle down Walker's spine.

"You wouldn't consider pressing charges for the assault? I know it's a while ago now, but we could reopen the case if –"

"And rake all that muck up again? No thanks. I've got two kids now, and a boyfriend that doesn't treat me like a punching bag."

"That's good. Can you think of anyone else that Paul might have been in contact with?"

"He has family somewhere in Scotland," she said, after a brief pause. "A cousin maybe? But apart from that I don't know. He never talked about his past. Should have been a clue. Look, I've got a client coming in for her nails. Got to go."

She hung up before Walker could ask anything else.

"Possible lead on Paul Cameron's family," Walker said, raising his voice so that the others could hear. "His ex-girlfriend reckons there might be a cousin in Scotland somewhere. Can we check it out?"

There was a collective nodding of heads and typing into the computers.

At that moment Macleod walked in. His stubble had got to a critical stage, as it always did at this point in an investigation. Walker wondered if it was because his wife was up in the Highlands and there was no one to tell him off. Or perhaps being a Detective meant that he didn't have to worry about such things. Another thing to recommend a move out of uniform, Walker thought.

"The Superintendent has got half the force out to search for

Cameron but still no sightings."

"We've just heard that he might have a cousin somewhere in Scotland," Walker said.

"Any idea where yet?"

"No. We just got the info from his ex-girlfriend. We're chasing it up just now."

Macleod folded his arms. "I hope we get him quickly. The press will be blaming us if he hurts anyone else after we released him."

Walker said nothing.

"The traffic cameras have him heading east out of Invergryff," Macleod said. "That could mean he's heading for this Scottish connection. Or it could mean he's off to England, then on to anywhere he wants in Europe."

"Unless we catch him."

Macleod didn't reply but his face said it all. Time was running out. Walker turned back to his computer. All they needed was a little bit of luck.

Chapter 23: Bernie

Bernie Paterson had always believed in making her own luck. Especially where the Wronged Women's Co-operative was concerned. When she had started the business, she had hustled her way to her first set of clients, making sure that everyone knew just how good she was. Now the clients found her, but Bernie still spent every moment of her free time thinking about the business.

And now she was losing Liz. Only for a while, of course, but Bernie knew that whatever her friend said, the baby would come first. And that was how it should be. But it left Bernie with a dilemma. For a while, she had thought Alice might become a partner in the business. She was family, after all. But when the girl had joined the Specials, Bernie knew it wasn't going to happen. And then there was Mary Plunkett. Brilliant, in a random, scatty sort of way, with loads of potential. But was she ready to step up to the mark?

To distract herself, Bernie set about cleaning the house, even though it was spotless as usual. She had just moved into the kitchen when the phone rang.

Bernie answered Liz's call on the first ring. "Is the baby here?"

"No," Liz said, in the tone of someone who had been asked the question several times that day. "I'm calling about something else."

"You need to make it quick," Bernie said, "I'm cleaning out

the cat litter so I've got you on speaker."

"Lovely. Look, I wanted to tell you about the chat I've just had with Dave."

"Is it about who does the nappies? Tell him he needs to do his share."

"That's all in hand, thank you very much," Liz replied.

Bernie grinned as she pulled on her rubber gloves and started the process of poop scooping. Sometimes it was too enjoyable to wind her friend up.

"All right, what was it you wanted then?"

"Alexander Guthrie was one of Dave's customers. He came in about a year ago with an injury to his eye that had happened at work. Nothing lasting, so Dave gave him a clean bill of health. But he says that Guthrie was worried about his wife finding out. He seemed particularly concerned about not having money coming in to keep her happy."

"I knew it!" Bernie would have pumped her fist only she had a bag of cat poo in that hand.

"Look, it doesn't prove anything, but it shows there was something weird going on in that marriage. If we add in the fact that when Mrs Guthrie was fired she didn't let her husband know, then it doesn't paint a great picture of life in that house. I hate to say it, Bernie, but you might be right about Annabel."

"Of course I was right." Bernie finished cleaning up and pulled her gloves off. "I don't suppose you fancy going round to her house?"

There was some muttering down the other end of the phone that Bernie couldn't quite make out.

"Dave says you're being ridiculous," Liz said, coming back to the speaker. "I'm due to go to the hospital tonight. But if I feel okay I'll try and fit in a visit to Mrs Guthrie."

"You're a star," Bernie said. "Keep your legs crossed for me," she added, then hung up the phone.

Witch the cat arrived to inspect the job.

"Clean enough for you?" Bernie asked, tickling her under the chin. Witch gave a 'wrowl' of approval.

Her son flopped into the kitchen and gave the cat a cuddle. At twelve he was in that strange state of almost teen-dom that meant he was grumpy and sweet in equal measures.

"Ready to go?" Bernie asked.

"Yeah. Can we pick up Jackson on the way?" Ewan asked.

"Sure." She watched him fuss the cat, who put up with it in a regal fashion, not showing too many signs that she was enjoying herself. Witch played an important part in the household. Bernie knew she was not the most demonstrative mother any child could hope to have. She wasn't like Mary Plunkett, all cuddles and crafts and banana bread. But she was a good parent in a lot of other ways, and if her son needed something soft and welcoming, there was always Witch.

They took the car to football practice, collecting Jackson on the way. As the two kids talked football players in the back, Bernie tried to work out what she was going to do about Annabel Guthrie. She needed to see the woman's phone. Or her computer. Something that would give her evidence that Mrs Guthrie wanted to kill her husband. But how exactly was she going to get it?

She dropped off the boys and sat in the carpark, staring out at nothing. Maybe she could persuade the police to look into it for her. They would be able to do so in a second, but there was no guarantee that they would share the information with her. Bernie thumped the steering wheel in frustration. She turned on the radio, hoping that it would calm her down.

"Members of the public are advised not to approach Paul Cameron but to notify their local police force if he is spotted…"

That's right, Cameron had gone missing. After Liz's phone call, Bernie had almost forgotten that the police had put out a statement looking for the man. Was Cameron the one that Mrs Guthrie had persuaded to knock her husband off the scaffolding for her? It seemed plausible. The man had struck her as violent and not too bright, which would be just the sort of person that Annabel would be able to manipulate.

Mind made up, Bernie started the engine. It didn't take long to drive to the Camerons' house as she already knew the way. Fifteen minutes later, Bernie chapped on their door. Alyssa Cameron answered, her face gaunt and her hair pulled into a greasy bun.

"I'm not talking to you," Alyssa said, only opening the door a few inches. "I've just got back from the police station and the social workers were around asking questions yesterday too. Haven't you harassed us enough?"

"I might just be able to help you," Bernie said. "And it doesn't look to me like you've got very many other friends."

"I have plenty of friends," Mrs Cameron said.

"That might have been true once. But I'm willing to bet you've got a lot less since you've been hanging out with Paul Cameron."

Alyssa folded her arms. "I get it. You're here to trash talk my husband so that I... what? Tell you that he killed that guy? He didn't, by the way."

"I'm not sure if he did or not," Bernie said. "In fact, I am known for my open mind. But the fact is that whether or not he killed Alexander Guthrie, the police can't move forward with the investigation until he's found. And neither can I."

Alyssa looked like she was about to burst into tears. Good, Bernie thought. It was about time the woman got a reality check and Bernadette Paterson was an expert at them.

"Look, the sooner you let me in, the sooner you can get rid of me."

That got her through the door. Alyssa led the way back into the kitchen that Bernie and Mary had been in so recently. It looked less perfect than it had before with dirty dishes in the sink and the bin needing emptied. Something else was missing too.

"Where's Sophia?"

"One of the mums from nursery has her. She just lives around the corner. It was... I told her there was a family emergency, but I think she might have already seen the news."

"You know that Paul is in a lot of trouble, right?"

"No one calls him that. He's Cammie," the woman sniffed.

"Right. Alyssa, what did Cammie do that made you move up here?"

"There was some trouble. A fight in a bar. Some guy attacked Cammie and he fought back. None of it was his fault. He hardly did any time. The judge could see he was a good guy."

Or there wasn't enough evidence to convict him of anything more serious, Bernie thought.

"But he does tend to be violent, doesn't he? I mean, I've already seen his temper."

Alyssa looked away for a split second, but that was enough.

"Cammie's good to me."

"Sure he is." Bernie checked the time on her phone. It was nearly lunchtime and she was meant to be meeting Mary. Probably not enough time to sort the snivelling woman's life out, but time enough to try.

"I wondered if I could tell you a little story," Bernie said.

"Is there anything I can do to stop you?"

"Nah. I'm like a vampire: once you let me in, that's it. Now you make us a cup of tea and I'll tell you this wee story."

Bernie watched as the woman put on the kettle and made the teas. She used full-fat milk, but sometimes even Bernie had to make sacrifices for the sake of the WWC.

"My friend Susan had a boyfriend once. A boyfriend just like Cammie. He was good to her too, until he wasn't."

"You never had a friend called Susan, did you?" Alyssa interrupted.

Bernie's eyes narrowed. "Yes, I did. And I had one called Tina and one called Fiona, and one called Bev too. And they all had the same bloody story. They stayed with a man that hit them until he hit them so hard that one day they left. The question isn't whether or not your man Cammie is hitting you. The question is: how hard does he have to hit you before you leave? Or does he have to hit your little girl first?"

The other woman gasped. "Cammie would never..."

"Tell that to the rest of them. The women with the same scared faces that you're wearing right now. How's it going to feel when he does hit Sophia and you didn't do anything to stop it?"

Bernie handed Alyssa a tissue.

"You're not... you're just as bad as the police, saying these things about him. That's not my Cammie."

If Bernie had been religious, she would have prayed for some tolerance. Or maybe the ability to sympathise with the woman, like Mary Plunkett would have done. As it was, all she had was the cold hard truth. "Look, I'm not asking you to dump his arse, although it'll be pretty clear to you that I think you should. All I'm asking is you tell me where he is."

"I don't know."

"Sorry pet but that's a load of bullcrap. When you watch every move that someone makes, like you do with your Cammie, just in case he turns nasty, you know where they go when they're in trouble."

"I don't like the way you talk about him. He's not some sort of monster."

"I know. That's what makes it worse."

"Look I –"

Bernie's patience, never exactly full to the brim, was wearing thin. She leaned across the table until she was right up in the woman's face.

"Tell me where he is and I'll leave you alone," she said gently. "Or don't tell me and I will haul you back to the police station myself."

"He's at his Aunt's place," Alyssa said, tears collecting in her eyes. "She stays just outside Falkirk."

"All right."

"And I will leave him," Alyssa said, her voice trembling as she said it.

Bernie squeezed her arm. "Good."

She left the house with a spring in her step. If Bernie had been Mary Plunkett then she would have believed Alyssa Cameron with absolute certainty when she had said she would leave her husband. But Bernie had seen a little more of life than Mary had and she reckoned it was more like fifty-fifty that Alyssa would go back to him.

But that was a better chance than there had been last night. And at least Bernie would improve her standing with the police as soon as she told them where the man was. She picked up her phone and called DI Macleod. She had already looked up his number, just in case.

Chapter 24: Liz

Liz's plan to go and visit Mrs Guthrie was dead in the water before it even started. When she drove up to the Guthrie house there was not one but two police cars outside. Bernie Paterson might have been able to claim she was a journalist to slip past them, but Liz reckoned being the size of your average sperm whale might make her a little too noticeable.

She left Mrs Guthrie's house and parked in a fast food restaurant car park, got herself a small bag of fries to munch on and called Dave. They had agreed she would check in every hour.

"I know I'm going to get it in the neck for this, but shouldn't you leave the others to it for now? I mean, given that you are going to have a baby this evening?"

Liz rolled her eyes. "I was going crazy in the house. I even considered watching Love Island."

Her husband laughed. "That is a bad sign. Do you want me to do anything to help?"

"No. Mrs Guthrie is a wash-out for now, unless Bernie can think of a clever way of getting her to talk to us. I'm going to chase up some of the other suspects. The police are still looking for Paul Cameron, so I'm going to look at the other people at the Abbey."

"You're going to go around and meet up with people you

might think are involved in a violent murder? And you could go into labour at any moment?"

Liz sighed. "How about I start with the women that work in the gift shop?"

"That sounds sensible to me," Dave replied.

When Liz got off the call with her husband she phoned the Abbey straight away, only to be told that Jodie from the gift shop hadn't been in for two days.

"She says she's sick," Mrs Button told her. "But I'm not so sure. Any excuse these youngsters find to take a day off. I've never had a sick day in my life."

"I don't doubt it," Liz replied. Luckily she already had the address for Jodie Green in her case file. It didn't take long to drive to the building. It was a block of flats in what used to be an old Victorian mill. They were very swanky, and Liz had fancied one for herself, when she was single and childless.

She parked the car and walked over to the entrance foyer. The buzzer system was clearly labelled and she pressed the one for Green.

"Hello?"

Liz said nothing. If there was one thing that she knew, it was that if you buzzed for long enough, someone would let you in.

"Hello?"

She started to hit all the buzzers. She had done half a dozen before someone got fed up and the security door clicked open.

It was entirely in keeping with the week that Liz was having that when she got to the stairwell the lift was broken and Jodie Green was on the sixth floor. By the time she had climbed the stairs, she was sweating with one hand on her lower back and one hand supporting her bump. She paused outside the door to get her breath back, then knocked.

"Jesus, are you okay?"

"I'm fine," Liz attempted a reassuring smile that came out as a grimace. "It's just a lot of stairs. Can I have a glass of water?"

"Uh, okay."

"I'm here to ask some questions about the death of Alexander Guthrie." Liz panted while the young woman handed her a glass.

"I thought you were a delivery. I'm expecting some new clothes."

Liz noticed that Jodie didn't seem to be very sick. She was wearing a hooded top and leggings and she looked like she might have just popped home from the gym. She made Liz feel even more like a mountain in human form.

"You were working on the day it happened, weren't you?"

Jodie sat down on her leather sofa and tucked her legs up under herself. The sofa was cream leather, the sort that had never once had a child put a sticky finger on it. The whole flat was like something out of a magazine with huge windows giving her a view of the town.

"Yeah, it was horrible. Me and Mrs Button were in the shop, you see, and we heard this like thump sound. That was AJ."

"Were you friends with Mr Guthrie?"

Jodie shrugged. "I saw him a few times a week when he came in to work. He seemed like an okay guy, but we weren't exactly mates or anything."

"This is a nice place," Liz said.

"Yeah, I like the view. I only moved in last summer."

"Must be expensive."

Jodie's eyes flickered down the way. "My parents help out."

Gotcha, Liz thought. It just so happened that she had taken a look at Jodie's credit history before she arrived. Working in a gift shop didn't exactly pay well, and the rent on this place had to be pushing four figures. Did she really just have generous parents?

"Mrs Button was telling me that you've not been back at work since the death of Alexander Guthrie."

"I've not been well," Jodie said, despite all evidence to the contrary.

"It must be a bit awkward though. I mean, people might think you have a guilty conscience or something."

Jodie wasn't stupid. She jumped up off the sofa. "Just what do you mean by that?"

"Like I said, a man is killed and then you avoid the place where it happened. Seems a bit funny to me, that's all."

"You can't just go around accusing people like that," Jodie said, her bottom lip curling downwards.

"If you wait until the police come knocking they're not going to be half as polite as me."

"You think the police will come here?"

"I know they will. They're not stupid and they know that something is going on. There's no way you can afford this flat on the wages you get from the gift shop. Someone's giving you money, and they're going to find out who."

Jodie put her fingers over her eyes. "What a mess."

Liz felt a kick under her ribs. She really needed to get out of there. "Look, I don't think you had anything to do with Guthrie's death. But I do think that you're protecting someone. Now, hadn't you better tell me who?"

Jodie said a name and then burst into tears. When she heard it, Liz wasn't one little bit surprised.

Five minutes later, Liz was on her way to the Abbey, having already texted Bernie and Mary to meet her there. She didn't realise until she pulled into the carpark that there was some sort of Church bake sale going on. She had to leave the car in a disabled spot. Not ideal but hopefully her bump would stop her from getting a ticket.

The stalls were all arranged on the grassy area outside the Abbey. A few people were browsing what seemed to be a lacklustre array of homemade candles and fudge. It took her a few minutes to see Bernie and Mary, deep in conversation at an ornamental woodwork stall.

"Oh god, are you still pregnant?" Bernie said as Liz came up beside them.

"Yes I am, and no I'm not bloody happy about it," she said, glaring at the two of them, and the world in general, for not being pregnant.

"What have the midwives said?"

"That I'm on the clock. I have to turn up for the induction in a couple of hours."

"Shouldn't you be relaxing until then?" Mary asked.

Liz didn't dignify that one with a reply. "Any sign of the man himself?"

"I asked Mrs Button and she said he was in the tea room," Mary said.

"I didn't know the Abbey had a tea room," Liz said.

"It's only open for a couple of hours a day," Bernie explained. "Typical Scottish attitude to tourists: give them the most beautiful building in the country but don't make it comfortable for them."

"All right, spare us the political insight," Liz said. "Let's go inside to the tea room."

"I heard that they have fresh scones," Mary added happily.

"We are not here for scones," Bernie said severely.

They walked through the main part of the Abbey to a newer section that housed the tea room.

"This place creeps me out," Bernie said, pulling her raincoat around her more closely.

"Creeps you out? Last time I was here someone dropped from the ceiling," Mary said and Liz noticed she was looking paler than usual. Her sombre face was an odd contrast to her 'Don't Hassel the Hoff' hoodie.

"Are you okay?"

"I will be when we get back outside. I've got my eye on some fudge. I just love a bake sale," Mary said with a faraway look on her face.

"I bet you do," Bernie said with a scowl.

"Don't have a fit, Bernie, it's all homemade."

"Oh, so the calories don't exist then? Sorry, I didn't realise being homemade meant that all the sugar simply evaporated."

Mary shrugged. "Your sarcasm does not offend me. I have future cakes to think of."

"I could buy some in for after the birth," Liz said. "Might be nice to have in the freezer."

"What about all those lentil casseroles I brought around for your freezer last week?" Bernie complained.

"Oh, they look fab," Liz said, which was not the word Dave had used when he had seen them. "But we'll need something for dessert as well. Anyway, let's focus on the task at hand. It's not going to be very nice."

The Reverend was sitting with a group of ancient-looking men in linen suits. He looked up when they entered and his face fell when he spotted Liz.

"Can I have a word," she asked as Bernie and Mary went to order teas.

"Not here," he said with a plaintive expression. "Come and meet me outside in five minutes."

Liz nodded in agreement. She signalled to the others that she would be back in a minute and then she went outside and browsed the stalls. She bought a small knitted gnome for Sean, mainly out of embarrassment that the tiny wizened stall holder clearly hadn't sold anything all day. After a few minutes, she went to find the man she was after.

The Reverend was sitting on a bench outside the Abbey. There were one or two graves scattered nearby, but it was mostly grass.

Liz sat down beside him. He didn't say a word, a tiny nod being the only acknowledgement of her existence.

"I found out where the money has been going."

"I thought you would. You seem like you know your business."

"I do," Liz said.

They sat together in silence for a few moments.

"Why are there so few graves out here?" Liz asked, filling the void.

"Because the Abbey has a crypt rather than a graveyard. Many did, in the past you see. Very practical."

Liz thought about the floor she had so recently walked over and wondered how many people were buried underneath. It gave her the shivers.

"Do you know Gray's Elegy? I often think of it when I sit here."

"Is that Elegy in a Country Churchyard?" Liz said, the name coming from somewhere deep in her memory. "I think we studied it in school."

"There will be no 'frail memorial' for me, will there? Not for the blushes of ingenuous shame. By lonely contemplation led, that's what Gray wrote. And instead of being led to a Churchyard, I was led here, to an Abbey with a crypt. And now you are going to lead me away, are you, Mrs Okoro?"

A tiny foot gave her a kick in the ribs, bringing Liz back to reality. "You can spout all the poetry you like, Reverend, but the fact remains that you used Church funds to pay for an affair with the woman who worked in the gift shop. Nothing poetic about that."

The Reverend sighed. "People have affairs all the time, of course."

"They do. And you might even have styled it out, if she was single. Only Jodie got married when she was twenty-one, didn't she? The sort of foolish decision that we sometimes make when we're young. The problem for you is that she never got divorced."

"She hasn't even seen him for a decade. Not that that will matter to the Church, of course. Have you told them already?"

"I thought you could tell them yourself. It might make them go easier on you."

The Reverend looked up at the clouds. "I don't think it will make a difference."

"No," Liz said, watching the bank of rain coming from the West. "I don't suppose it will."

Chapter 25: Mary

Mary had left the final interrogation of the Reverend to Liz. She knew that her friend was tougher than she was. The moment she had seen the man's hangdog expression and watery eyes, Mary knew she would be far too soft on him. After all, it was an affair, not murder.

While Liz was outside, Mary walked around the interior of the Abbey. It was strange being back. No, it was awful being back. There were still the leftover pieces of police tape flickering around the centre of the Abbey where the man had died. If Mary closed her eyes she knew she would be able to picture his body, lying there. Still warm.

She shuddered. Wasn't there some Eastern proverb about if you saw a man die you owed him something? Maybe it was just something from a Jackie Chan movie. Whichever it was, Mary had never felt more determined to uncover Guthrie's killer than when she stood on those old stone slabs looking at the place where he had died.

"Time for a cuppa, dear?" Mrs Button had appeared by her side out of nowhere.

"Sure," Mary said with a smile.

"Then let's sneak into the staff room for a bit."

They walked through the tiny gift shop to an even tinier staff room that only had room for two chairs, a small round table and the tea making things.

"I won't even charge you for it," Mrs Button said as she poured Mary a cup of strong sweet tea.

"My friend Liz is outside talking to the Reverend," Mary said.

"Is she the pregnant lady? She's positively glowing!"

"I'll tell her that. I don't think she feels like there's much of a glow. She's due in for an induction today."

"God's finest miracle," Mrs Button said, looking every inch the kindly old lady. "There's nothing more glorious than a newborn child."

"I agree," Mary answered. "Liz is here to ask the Reverend about Jodie."

"Ah." Mrs Button pursed her lips together.

"You knew, of course."

"Of course. People think they are so clever when they have these sordid little affairs. But they never are. It's easy enough to tell if you've been around the block a few times, and believe me I have."

"You didn't report him to the Church?"

"Cast the first stone? No, I believe in Christian charity."

"Did you know he was siphoning off Church funds to pay for it all? The hotel rooms, the little gifts… they all add up."

Mrs Button shivered. "No, I did not know that. Silly man. There's none so foolish as an old man whose head has been turned by a young woman. And I never liked that girl. She didn't sweep the floor properly. There were always dust bunnies in the corners. And now she'll have to find another job. Well, at least the new girl can work the till."

"The Reverend couldn't have had anything to do with Alexander Guthrie's death, could he?"

Mrs Button shook her head. "Reverend McDade is a weak man. That Jodie set her sights on him and that was it. But murder someone? Lay his hands on another person in violence? No, he would never do that."

Mary took a sip of her tea. "I'm afraid that our investigation isn't going very well. My friend Bernie thinks that the wife is the most likely suspect, but I can't see her climbing up the scaffolding to push her husband off."

"It would be much easier to poison him at home," Mrs Button suggested.

"Quite. In terms of opportunity, the other stonemasons look most likely. And Paul Cameron has done a runner, so that makes him the number one suspect as far as the police are concerned. But I just can't see a motive."

"Money or sex. That's normally the motive. I learned that on the True Crime channel."

Mary smiled. "You could be right. Unless it's the wife, I can't see how sex comes into it. We haven't seen any sign that

Guthrie was having an affair."

"Then it's probably all about money."

"I agree. My friend Liz has a certain ability with bank accounts, so we're still looking into it. You didn't see anyone giving Guthrie any cash? Or the other way around?"

"No, sorry dear."

"And there was nothing strange about that day. Nothing that he did differently?"

"No."

"Did he know about the Reverend and Jodie?"

"I don't think so. Although… he did say something funny one day. I was talking to him about the Reverend and how his last sermon had gone. Say what you like about the man, he was a fine speaker in the pulpit. And the reading was from the book of John and Guthrie must have caught the end of the service because he came over and asked me about it."

"Did he? I didn't realise Guthrie was a religious man."

"I don't think he was. But you know the verses from John are rather catchy. Very quote-worthy as the youngsters would say."

Mary wasn't sure the youngsters would say anything of the sort. "Can you remember exactly what the Reverend had said that day?"

"He was quoting the part about forgiveness. 'If we say we

have no sin we deceive ourselves'. It's about the need for confession."

"And Guthrie was interested in that?"

"Very. He asked me if I thought it was true that there could be no forgiveness without confession. And I said of course it was true. Self-evident, really. And that seemed to make him pause for thought. Then he thanked me and went back to work."

Mary felt a little out of her depth. Religious verses were not exactly my area of expertise.

"Why did you think he was so struck by those verses?" Mary asked Mrs Button.

The older woman sighed. "At the time, I assumed he must have something he needed to confess."

"Any idea what?"

"None whatsoever."

Chapter 26: Walker

The police station was full of worried faces. After Bernie had called them, Macleod had acted on the lead that Paul Cameron might be at his Aunt's house. She lived in a small village called Loanhead, just outside Falkirk. A team had been sent to keep an eye on her cottage and see if there was any sign of the man. Until they called back, Cameron was officially still in the wind.

"It's going to be a right balls-up for us if we don't find him soon," Macleod said, his hang-dog expression even worse than usual. "The Superintendent has asked for hourly updates, but I've nothing to tell him."

Walker's phone pinged with a message. "Dr Burrell has just sent me a message asking if we want to come down to the lab. He's got some news on the fingerprints at the crime scene."

Macleod stood up immediately, like he was glad of the distraction. "Let's go check it out."

The forensics lab was a new addition to Invergryff police station. It was only a couple of rooms on the second floor which had been used for storage until recently. But as part of a new Government scheme there had been a decentralisation of the forensics department which had normally all been sent off to the capital. Now the larger police stations were getting their very own forensics departments, even if they were somewhat bijou.

"Come in," Dr Burrell said when they knocked on the door.

"I'll have my secretary make you a coffee. Oh, that's right, she's still in Edinburgh, along with the rest of my staff."

Rumour had it that Dr Burrell was not very happy about the move out of Headquarters.

"We're not here for coffee," Macleod said. "You've got some information on the fingerprints from our crime scene?"

Burrell hauled his skinny frame out of his chair and led them through to the lab. "Yes, that's right. I've got it all set up for you."

It was very strange to see the upper section of scaffolding in the middle of the forensics lab, covered in plastic sheeting.

"I would appreciate it if you could wrap this case up soon," Dr Burrell said. "I normally have my desk in that space."

"We're doing our best," Macleod said with a glare at the doctor.

"I wanted to talk you through the fingerprints. It may take a while."

"We are very busy trying to find a suspect," Macleod grumbled.

Dr Burrell gave him a sharp look. "Then you'll want to do so with all the facts, won't you?"

"Of course."

Walker had the feeling that Burrell had won that round.

"Can we talk about fingerprint placements?" Burrell said, pulling off the plastic to expose the scaffolding.

"Sure," Macleod said, although Walker could tell the Inspector was getting frustrated. Dr Burrell liked to take his time getting to the point.

Burrell began pointing at the pieces of metal. "We're looking at the top level of the scaffolding here, and this point here is where we believe Alexander Guthrie fell from. Scuff marks on the wooden boards are consistent with this hypothesis. Now, let's consider the fingerprints. I've highlighted all the prints we've got here. I've marked Guthrie's with the red tabs, Cameron's with the yellow, Finlayson's with the blue."

Walker peered closer to see the markers.

"Cameron's are all on the right-hand side of the scaffolding. He was the specialist, remember? So he's working on this ornate section over here. The other two were the general stonemasons, they were doing the repairs to the arch."

"What does that mean?" Walker asked.

"If we look at the fingerprints, Cameron wasn't up the end of the scaffolding where Guthrie was pushed. But Finlayson was."

"We can get Finlayson back in," Macleod said. "But there's no way to prove that those fingerprints came from the day of the murder, is there?"

"No."

"So Cameron is still our most likely suspect, despite the fingerprint evidence. What if he wore gloves?"

"Possible." Burrell nodded. "All the stonemasons would have worn industry gloves when working with concrete and so on. But from what I gather, they often do the most intricate work with their bare hands."

"But if they were planning on killing someone?"

"Then they might have had gloves on."

Macleod rubbed a hand over his face. "Then it doesn't really discount anyone, does it?"

Dr Burrell held out his arms. "Welcome to forensics."

Chapter 27: Bernie

The knowledge that they had found a cheating Reverend and yet not been paid for the work was irking Bernie. Normally affairs were the biggest earner for the WWC. They had to stop these investigations that they were doing for free. Just as soon as they proved that Annabel Guthrie had killed her husband.

Bernie needed to speak to Mrs Guthrie. She needed to see the whites of her eyes. But to do that she would have to find a way past the police cars that had been stationed at the Guthrie house ever since the murder. It was time for her to burn her bridges with the police. In point of fact, Bernie thought, she had never really built any bridges with them in the first place. But no matter, it was time to tear up any agreement that there had been between the WWC and the local constabulary.

It might cause a slight issue for Mary Plunkett and her blossoming relationship with Sergeant Walker, but if they couldn't withstand a little professional enmity then they weren't much good for one another in the first place.

Finn was at work and Ewan was at a friend's house for a sleepover so there was no one at home to tell her not to drive to Annabel Guthrie's house. Now that she knew there would be a police presence at the house, Bernie made sure to park two streets away. She pulled on her running gear and one of Finn's old hoodies, making sure that the hood was pulled low over her face.

She got out of the car, grabbed a bucket she had placed there earlier and started to jog. Bernie loved running. She didn't mind the gym, but it was something that she endured rather than enjoyed. Running, on the other hand, moving your way along the road with a purpose in mind, that was when she felt truly free.

But today she had a different plan. She turned up the street that was just before the one that the Guthries lived on. Luckily, it was a housing estate with cookie-cutter houses and gardens. Bernie ran along for a short time before she found a house roughly in line with Mrs Guthries. The first one had two cars in the drive, so she ruled that out. The next had no cars and when she rang the bell there was no one home. Perfect. She took a scrim and a sponge out of the bucket and started to clean the windows.

No one noticed her. It was going to be the perfect heist. After a few minutes, she pulled open the gate to the back garden and let herself in. From here she could see the back of Annabel Guthrie's house, just one house along on the right. Bernie took out her phone. It was important to move quickly.

"Hello, is this the emergency gas line? I want to report a leak."

It only took twenty minutes for the gas vans to turn up, particularly as Bernie had explained just how strong the smell of gas was from the neighbouring house to Mrs Guthrie's. Luckily, the garden that Bernie was currently in was on a slight incline so she could see across through the gaps in the fence. Two vans and several worried-looking men in high-vis vests arrived.

If Bernie knew anything about people it was that they had more in common than they were different. And she knew that if there was any sort of commotion it was a universal human need to go out and have a right good nosy at it.

From her vantage point, she couldn't tell if all the police officers had left the Guthrie house to find out what was happening on the street, but she would just have to chance it. Bernie used all her pull-up abilities to scramble over the fence and into the Guthries' garden. From there it was a quick crouching run to the back door.

Someone up there was smiling down on Bernie because when she touched the handle the door opened. She made a mental note to have a little word with Sergeant Walker about his fellow officer's security arrangements. The back door led directly into the kitchen and for a moment Bernie stood there, frozen to the spot. She could hear voices at the front door, presumably the police officers chatting to the gas men.

This was the most dangerous bit. Luckily, the stairs were in the middle of the house, leading off the living room, not the hallway. Bernie crept through to the living room. Empty. Heart pounding she raced for the stairs. She made her way up them as silently as possible, being careful to stand on the edges in case they creaked.

At the top of the stairs, she took a breath. Made it. All the bedroom doors were shut and Bernie guessed that Mrs Guthrie was behind one of them. But which one? Sod it, she just had to guess.

Bernie pulled a door open and slipped inside. For a moment

she was in darkness until her hand scrabbled and found the light switch. Which revealed a rather small family bathroom.

"Crap."

Somehow, this wasn't how she had imagined things going. This sort of thing had never happened to George Clooney in that Casino. She was just deciding what to do next when the door opened and someone came in.

"What the hell are you doing in my loo?" Annabel Guthrie said, her mouth falling open.

"Give me a minute to explain."

"Why should I? I'm going to yell for the police right now."

"Don't you dare," Bernie grabbed something in desperation and waved it at the woman.

"Are you threatening me with a toilet brush?"

Bernie looked down at the object that had appeared in her hand.

"Yuck!" She put it back in the holder. "Look, you can call the police if you like. But I'm here to find out once and for all whether or not you killed your husband. Do I look like the sort of person who is just going to give up if you get me arrested?"

"You look like a psychopath. In my bathroom."

"I don't find labels very helpful," Bernie said with a sniff. "The police are looking for Paul Cameron. They're going to find him too. So I want you to explain why you had him kill your husband."

Mrs Guthrie frowned. "What rubbish is this? I barely knew Paul Cameron."

"You weren't having an affair?"

"No. Why would I? That Cameron bloke was a creep."

Funny, there was something about the disgust on Annabel Guthrie's face that made Bernie think she might be telling the truth. But that didn't make sense.

"You were in this up to your neck, weren't you?"

"What do you mean?"

Bernie felt like she was Jeremy Paxman, firing off questions that the other woman couldn't answer.

"What about the secret bank accounts?" Bernie asked, bringing out the big guns. "Was that how you hid your affairs?"

Now the woman did look worried as she backed up against the shower cubicle.

"What bank accounts?"

"My friend is an accountant. She took a look at all your credit files. You had a whole load of credit cards and savings accounts that were separate from your husbands. Some of these had some regular, high value deposits going into them."

"They have nothing to do with Alexander's death. And if you

tell the police about them, then I swear I will kill you."

"Like you killed Alexander?"

"You bloody stupid woman, I didn't kill my husband."

"You arranged for him to be killed then, it's hardly any different."

"What? No! Look, will you just shut your trap and listen for a minute?"

For once, Bernie did as she was told.

"I didn't kill him, but I know who did. Because I was blackmailing them."

Now this had the ring of truth. "Explain it to me. Now."

"It started a few weeks ago. Well, part of it did anyway. Alexander remembered something he had seen ages ago. At the time it hadn't really mattered, but something made him rethink it. Anyway, he told me all about it, wanted to go to the police, all sorts. I told him just to keep quiet, and that spilling other people's secrets was never a good idea."

"What was the secret?"

"You expect me to tell you that? Give you the proof that I was blackmailing someone so you can take it to the police? I am not going to jail for this."

"All right then," Bernie said, thinking tactically, "tell me enough to convince me that you didn't kill your husband and I might just forget about the blackmail thing."

"All right. When Alex told me about what he'd seen, I knew there was money in it somewhere."

"That's where the blackmail came in?"

Annabel nodded. "Alexander was so tight with his money, and I needed some cash. I'd booked a couple of holidays that he didn't know about and I'd already maxed out my credit cards. I asked him if he could share some of his spare pay, but he said it was all for his pension. What utter crap. He just didn't want me to have any. So this was a way to get some money for myself. And I knew that I could pull it off so that he never even found out about it."

"So what went wrong?"

"I wrote an email to this... person with a secret. I told them that I knew all about it, but that I would keep my mouth shut for a certain amount of money."

"How much?"

"Five grand."

"Was it Cameron? Or Finlayson?"

"Neither of them," she said, but Bernie wasn't convinced. "Anyway, it doesn't matter who it was. My point was, I had no reason to kill my husband, but someone else did."

"Why would they kill your husband, and not you?"

She rubbed her eyes. "Because I used his laptop to send the demands. I thought I had it covered by using a throwaway email address, but they must have worked it out somehow. Alexander was thrown off the roof the day after I asked for the money."

This had the ring of truth about it. Bernie crossed her arms. "All right, I believe that you didn't kill him. But you need to speak to the police. You have to tell them who killed your husband."

"I'll just deny it all. Hell, I shouldn't even have told you, only I need to get you off my back. I'm sick of the sight of your moany little face. Just like in school, always popping up where you're not wanted."

It was Bernie's turn to gasp. "You remember me?"

"You were a bit too big to forget, weren't you?"

Bernie swallowed. "I'm an investigator now."

"Poking around in other people's lives rather than living your own. You know, if it weren't for the fact that you were thick-as-a-plank, fat Bernie from school then I would be shouting out to the police right this moment. But I know that you are so obsessed with me that you're going to do what I tell you. And that is to get lost."

There were a hundred things Bernie wanted to say to Annabel at that moment, but what would any of them prove? Nothing. And most likely only make her shout out for the police officers downstairs.

"This isn't personal, Annabel," Bernie said slowly, forcing the words to come out in a calm voice. "I want to find out who killed your husband. And if you're telling me the truth that you didn't kill him..."

"I am."

"Then I'll never have to speak to you again. I've got everything I need now. Give me five minutes, then I'll sneak out the back."

"Fine," Annabel said. "I hope I never see you again."

"Feeling's mutual," Bernie replied as the door closed behind her. Five minutes later she managed to escape the house without being seen. When she got back to her car she slumped into the seat. It was going to take a minute to digest what Annabel had just told her. And the fact that she had remembered her. Bernie was disappointed that the woman wasn't going to jail for murder, but she would make sure that she got her for the blackmail, one way or the other. At that moment, however, she would just have to comfort herself with the fact that she had had just enough time to run Annabel Guthrie's toothbrush around the bowl of the toilet. It was the little things in life that mattered.

Chapter 28: Liz

Liz was at Bernie's house. She hadn't taken her coat off as she was determined not to stay long. Dave had been less than impressed that she wasn't heading straight home after the Abbey, but Bernie had been buzzing to tell her something over the phone. Liz had barely got in the door before her friend told her about breaking into Mrs Guthrie's home.

"You're completely insane, you do realise that don't you?" Liz said.

Bernie grinned. "Yep. And now we know what the woman was up to."

"But she wouldn't tell you who she was blackmailing?"

"No. I think it might have been more than one person. But she said it wasn't Finlayson or Cameron."

"That's if she's telling the truth."

"Yeah. The thing is, the evidence points to one of them. She's not stupid though, our Annabel. She knows that if she tells the police about the blackmail she'll be facing charges herself, even if it clears her of the murder. That's why she wouldn't give me a name."

"And there's not much point in us telling them until we've worked out exactly who she's been blackmailing."

"That's why I need your computer skills. Can you trace the

money?"

Liz frowned. "Not without full access to her accounts, and I can't do that by myself."

"I had a feeling you might say that," Bernie looked disappointed. "I'm going to have a gin, then I'm going to call Mary. Maybe she'll have some ideas. Do you want a gin?"

Honestly, sometimes the woman was something else. Liz pointed at her belly. "I'm about to be induced, Bernie."

"Probably good for pain relief," Bernie said with a shrug.

For a moment, Liz was almost tempted. Then she thought of what the midwives would say if she went in stinking of booze. "Just a glass of water please."

"Maybe we should just go and see Finlayson," Bernie said, pouring a decent measure of gin into the glass.

Liz felt a twinge in her back and thought the baby was moving around again. She expected it to go away after a couple of seconds, but it didn't. If anything it got worse.

"Oh no," she whispered, just as the pain disappeared. It was probably nothing. Those Braxton Hicks things that people always talked about. Absolutely nothing to worry about.

"Are you okay?" Bernie asked.

Liz gave her a wide grin. "Fine. What was that about Finlayson?"

"Well, the police are going to track down Cameron any time

now, and when they do they'll have him shut up tight in the police station so that he doesn't scarper again. So Finlayson is the only one that we can get at right now."

"Oof!" Liz said as another shudder of pain moved its way across her back.

"What was that?"

"Um… I think it was a contraction."

Bernie's eyebrows shot up her forehead. "You're kidding, right?"

"Not really," Liz said, trying to catch her breath.

"Maybe it's just a false alarm."

"I don't think so." Another contraction had her gritting her teeth and making a weird low humming noise.

"Bloody hell, Liz, you're meant to be induced tonight. We have almost got this murder all wrapped up. This is not a convenient time!"

"Well I'm very sorry about that," Liz said, closing her eyes as another wave of pain arrived.

"Let me get my phone," Bernie said. "I'll call Dave."

"Tell him to meet me at the maternity suite."

"He's not answering."

"Typical."

"I'll send him a message."

Liz shut her eyes as Bernie tapped away on her phone.

"How close together are the contractions?"

"Too blooming close. I need to get to the hospital."

Bernie banged her fist on the kitchen counter. "This is the last thing I need."

Liz gasped as a twinge of pain arched through her lower back. "Me too!"

"You know that the killer is about to be caught right at this moment. And the police have every chance of getting there first if we don't do something right now."

"Bernie, I need you to think about this. You can't expect me to have a baby in your kitchen just because you want to take down a murderer. You need to choose me over the case."

Liz gasped as Bernie reached over and grabbed her chin. The other woman stared into her eyes and Liz was too terrified to blink.

"Have you lost control of your senses as well as your pelvic floor?" Bernie hissed. "Of course I'm choosing you. I've just texted Mary and Walker about the blackmail. They can get the murderer themselves. No case is worth more than the WWC's second most important member."

"Then what…"

"I just wanted you to appreciate what I'm missing out on. An honest-to-god murder conviction. And this glass of gin that I haven't even had a chance to taste. Now let's get this show on the road."

They climbed into Bernie's car, Liz gritting her teeth with every movement. It would have been nice if the tyres had screeched as they pulled out onto the main road just for dramatic effect. Unfortunately, it was the part of Invergryff that had the most traffic calming measures so instead the only sound was that of their bums smacking down on their seats every time Bernie raced over a sleeping policeman.

By the time they got to the maternity hospital, Liz had her eyes screwed shut and was trying desperately to breathe between contractions. Bernie kept informing her about which stage her cervix must be at, and this was not helping her relax.

They entered the maternity ward and Bernie explained the situation to the nurses on duty.

"They're going to take you to the general ward, then they'll give you an exam to see how far along you are."

"Right." Liz realised she should know all this from her first labour, but the panic that had set in when the contractions started had forced all her knowledge out of her brain.

"Where's Dave?"

"No sign yet."

"Bloody hell, Berns, he's not going to miss it, is he?"

"Have a drink of water." Bernie handed her a plastic cup of

water which Liz did her best to sip. "If Dave doesn't come, I'll stay. Be your birth partner, or whatever it's called."

"Really?"

"I'm not going to leave you on your own, am I?"

Liz fought for the words to say, but she couldn't quite find them.

Then the door banged open.

"Sorry, I was on a work call. I came as soon as I got your message."

Lovely, lovely Dave with his worried face and his hands full of bags.

"Are you okay?"

"Yes, they're just finding me a room. The contractions have settled down to three minutes apart."

"Good," Dave said. "I brought all your things."

"I'll be off now," Bernie said, taking a step backwards.

Liz grabbed Bernie into a great big hug. "Thank you."

Her friend blinked furiously. "Don't be a wet lettuce. I'll see you soon."

Chapter 29: Mary

Mary was waiting for Walker to come over. After the confrontation with the Reverend and all the excitement about the Abbey case, she had barely had time to think about the conversation with her mother all day. But now that Liz and Bernie had gone home and Nel had taken the kids around to her house for the night, there was nothing to do but think.

Walker would have mentioned it if he wanted a child, wouldn't he? That was the thought that Mary was clinging to. Because she knew in her heart that she didn't want any more kids. And it wouldn't be fair to have another baby unless it was one hundred per cent wanted. That was something she would not compromise on.

So where would that leave them if Walker did want a baby? With nowhere to go, that was where. Mary reached for the pack of chocolate bars she kept hidden from the kids at the back of the cupboard. Weren't relationships meant to get easier as you got older? She hadn't had this sick feeling in her stomach since the love of her life had dumped her at age fourteen after she had made him a mix-tape. Apparently he wasn't into S Club 7. His loss.

It was time to get her game face on. Walker had said he would stop by after work, and if they were going to have a serious conversation about their relationship then she needed to look at her cutest. She pulled on her least grubby pair of leggings and a tunic top that skimmed over her mum tum. And her necklace that said 'Donald Trump is my b*tch' because Walker always said it made him laugh.

It wasn't long before the doorbell rang. Mary checked her reflection in the hall mirror. Make-up okay, hair no more mad than usual. She opened the front door with a smile.

"I wanted to have a word with you." Paul Cameron said.

For a moment, she couldn't think of anything to say.

"Why are you here?" Mary managed to whisper.

"Like I said, I wanted a word with you. Just like you invited yourself into my house, see?"

This was very bad, Mary thought. She didn't like the smug smile on his face one little bit.

"I don't think you should come in," Mary said, standing her ground.

"It's funny that you think you have a choice," Cameron said and then he gave the door a shove. She staggered backwards and before she realised what was happening the man was inside the house, locking the door behind him.

This can't be happening, Mary thought. It was like something out of a nightmare. She backed into the kitchen.

"Give me your phone. I don't want you calling anyone."

Walker! He said he would come over, but when? She prayed he would turn up soon.

Cameron held out his hand and she took out her phone and handed it to him. She hated seeing it disappear into his pocket, but she didn't have much choice. It seemed wise not to antagonise him. How far was he willing to go?

"How did you find out where I live?" Mary asked. Keep him talking, she thought. Isn't that what they always saw in the movies?

"Wasn't that hard. Alyssa knew someone that had kids at your school. She asked around. It's funny, you know, maybe I should be the investigator?"

She would almost have felt better if he was smashing the place up. But the cold calm expression on his face was scaring her more than anything. The only thought that Mary could cling to was: thank god the children are at their gran's house.

"You're only going to cause yourself more trouble being here. The police are already looking for you."

"They think I killed Guthrie. And I wonder who told them that?"

Mary's back was against the kitchen counter. There was nowhere else to go. "I didn't tell them that you killed anyone. We're still conducting the investigation."

"But you did get in touch with your little friend at social work, didn't you?"

Bloody hell. "I don't know what you mean," Mary said.

"Must be a coincidence then. Two women I've never met

before make themselves at home in my house and then the next day someone is asking me questions about my 'anger management issues'."

Oh God. She had called her friend at social work as soon as they had left the Camerons' place that day. It had been the memory of little Sophia playing on her slide while her dad shouted at them in the kitchen. How had he found out? Or was it just a lucky guess?

"I don't know what you mean. Look, I'm an investigator. I work for a Detective Agency. That's why I was there. I was just doing my job."

"So you do your job and next thing someone takes my kid off me? That's not going to happen."

Mary felt her heart thump in her chest. She was sure it was going far too fast to be healthy. "It's clear that you love your daughter," she said. "But I don't think breaking into people's homes is a very good way of showing it."

He slammed a fist down on the kitchen table. The chocolate bars scattered all over the floor. "You really think you can tell me what to do? Bitch!"

Mary flinched at the word. She could see he was on the verge of losing it completely. The kids' tablet was on the table, half-covered by a book of word searches. She could use it to call someone, couldn't she? But how would she get to it?

It was so hard to think when she was scared. What would Bernie do? Mary knew that her friend would make short work of the intruder.

But Mary was not Bernie. She was not tough. She was a wet lettuce and she was trapped in her house with a potential murderer. What on earth was she going to do?

"Would you... like a cup of tea?"

Cameron's eyes nearly popped out of his head. "A cup of tea? Are you kidding?"

"You came here to talk, didn't you?" Please god let him have come here to talk and not to hurt me, Mary thought. "So maybe we should drink tea like civilised people."

Cameron didn't say anything. Mary took a step towards the kettle, then another one. After all, he wasn't armed. He crossed his arms and Mary saw the size of his muscles. Damnit, he didn't need to be armed if he could choke the life out of her.

Just breathe. Mr Hoppy, Johnny's plastic rabbit looked at her from the draining rack. It was just all so unreal. The kettle boiled and she took two mugs out of the cupboard, her hands shaking.

"What do you take in your tea?" Mary asked, forcing the words out of her tight throat.

"Milk and two," Cameron said.

She almost laughed at how ridiculous it was.

He cracked his knuckles and she tried not to wince. "I guess you know the police are looking for you."

"I'm all over the papers," he said in disgust. "Someone's fitting me up for this murder."

"You didn't do it?"

"No. Should have done though. That bastard Guthrie was blackmailing me."

Bernie had sent Mary a message about blackmail earlier, but Mary had thought it was the wife, not the dead man that had been demanding money. But it was too hard to think about the details now with the adrenaline flowing through her body.

"That's a motive, isn't it? Blackmail?"

"It would have been, if I'd known it was him. I just got a message from an unknown number saying that I had better pay them five hundred quid or they would tell the Reverend about the assault charge."

"Did you pay it?"

"Yes. And then good old Guthrie gets murdered and I start thinking: what sort of guy gets pushed off the scaffolding? The sort that takes money off the wrong people, that's who."

"But it wasn't you?"

"No."

Mary breathed out. The two cups of tea were still sitting on the counter, untouched. "I could tell them that. I mean, as an official investigator. They'll listen to me when I say that you didn't do it."

Cameron looked away and Mary could see the muscles clenched in his jaw. He reached out to one of the kitchen shelves and took down a framed picture.

"Nice kids," he said, and that was it. That was the moment. Mary had never felt anger like it. She thought it might explode out of her and she bit down on her tongue to stop from screaming. How dare he mention her kids!

"I came here to teach you a lesson," he said, his voice low and mean. "And that's what I'm going to do. And then afterwards, you're going to tell the police that I didn't kill Guthrie. Because if you don't I'm going to come after your kids."

Mary could hardly breathe.

"I won't hurt you too badly. Not anywhere that shows. I'll just put the fear of God into you. Teach you a little lesson on how a woman should behave."

Although she knew it was coming, she only just had time to turn her back as he pressed his fingers into her throat. But she wasn't scared any more. Only angry. Mary grabbed Mr Hoppy and whacked Cameron over the head as hard as she possibly could.

Cameron staggered backwards, knocking plates and cups over as he fell. He fell to the floor groaning in pain. Mary turned back to the cupboards and reached up to where she kept the knives, well out of reach of the children but right where she needed them. The carving knife felt just right in her palm.

"I'm a good cook," she said, panting just a little. "And I keep my knives nice and sharp. You don't want to try touching me again."

"All right, all right. Just don't stab me, okay?" Blood was running down his forehead and he blinked to keep it out of his eye.

The front door banged open and Mary flinched, but she didn't let go of the knife. It was like she was watching a movie, standing above herself when Walker ran in with two more police officers and dragged Cameron to his feet.

One of the officers recited the police caution while another placed the handcuffs on Cameron's wrists.

"Mary, it's all right. You can put that down now."

She felt a gentle pressure as Walker took the knife from her hand. Next thing she knew she was pressed into his chest, tears rolling down her face.

Ten minutes later they were both on the sofa, fresh cups of tea in their hands.

"We clocked Cameron's van coming back into Invergryff," Walker explained. "At first we thought he was going home. I never thought for a moment…"

Mary could see he was struggling to speak.

"I didn't think he'd come here either," she said softly. "But I'm all right."

"When I saw his van outside, I thought you were… God, it was the worst moment of my life."

"I know. And all because I contacted social work about the kid. I shouldn't have got involved. You can say I told you so if you like."

Walker's mouth hung open for a second. Then he pulled her into his arms and held her so tight she thought he might crack a rib.

"Are you crazy? I'm not going to tell you off. I'm just glad you're okay. I was so worried."

"It was all right in the end," Mary said. "I mean, he talked a big talk, but I'm not sure he would actually have hurt me."

"We found his ex-girlfriend," Walker said, his voice cold. "She had to have her jaw wired after the last time Cammie lost his temper."

"Jesus." Mary wiped her eyes. "Did you tell Alyssa about that?"

"Yes. She's taken the kid and gone to stay with her mum."

"Well, that's something."

"What do you want to do now?" Walker said.

Mary managed a smile. "I want to give my kids a hug. Then I want to find out who killed Alexander Guthrie and be done with this case once and for all."

Chapter 30: Walker

Sergeant Walker had never been a violent man. Which was a funny thing to say about someone that had been in both the army and the police force. But the reason why he had been good at both jobs was that he had always been good at controlling his temper. But when he had seen Paul Cameron in Mary's house, he had almost lost it.

His mind was still filled with images of punching Cameron's lights out, long after the man had been taken away in the police van. He'd had to get the other police officers to bring him in or Cameron would have found himself suffering a nasty fall in the van.

And here was Mary, sitting with her cup of tea just like normal and her bravest face on. It was almost too much to bear. Walker wasn't used to this level of raw emotion. It was threatening to overwhelm him. He looked out of the window for a minute, just to get his breath back.

"I had almost forgotten," Mary said, turning to face him. "There was something I wanted to ask you about. Sam Finlayson's wife died in a car crash, right?"

Walker nodded. "Yes. A year or so ago. It was an accident."

"The rumour going around was that she was drunk behind the wheel."

"I only glanced at the reports before we brought Finlayson in for questioning, but from what I remember there was a half-empty bottle of vodka in the car. There was no other vehicle involved and the suggestion was that she was drunk-driving."

"Was alcohol found in her body post-mortem?"

"I'd have to check. Why?"

"A loose end. My mother was talking about the Finlaysons and she said that Ginny wasn't drinking. She was on a diet at the time."

"Doesn't sound like conclusive evidence to me. Maybe she just fell off the wagon for a night."

"Cameron said he didn't kill Guthrie. He even admitted he was being blackmailed. For a guy like that, to admit to loss of face… I believed him. I think we need to look at Finlayson again."

Walker wasn't sure he agreed, but at that moment he would do anything Mary asked. "I'll ask the guys in the office to check it out."

"Will you do it now?"

"Okay." He didn't like leaving her even to walk out of the room. Constable Harrow was in the kitchen, taking some preliminary photos before the forensics guys turned up.

"Lucky we came when we did," Harrow said, taking a picture of the mess.

"Lucky my girlfriend is a badass," Walker replied. He took out his phone and dialled the station.

Neil picked up on the first ring. "Cameron's just arrived. We've got him safely locked up and he'll be in the interview room as soon as we get him a solicitor. How's Mary?"

"Coping better than me," Walker said with a chuckle.

"I'll bet."

"Cameron was telling her that he didn't kill Guthrie."

"Well, he would say that, wouldn't he?"

Walker found himself agreeing, but he had made a promise to Mary to check out every possibility, let alone the need to do his job well. "Can we take another look at Finlayson? Did he ever give a reason for coming to the Abbey on Sunday when he told us he was nowhere near?"

"Said he had to grab some tools. Never went near the scaffolding."

"So why lie?"

"Nerves apparently."

"Huh. Anyone back up his story?"

"Not as far as I know but I can double-check."

"While you're at it, will you have a look into the death of his wife?"

"That was the car crash, right? I thought it was an accident."

"The rumour was she was drunk, but Mary reckons she was off the booze at the time. It's probably nothing, but worth going back over the files."

"I'll check them out. Give your missus a hug for me."

"Will do."

He went back into the living room where Mary was grabbing her handbag.

"Did you pack up some overnight things for your mum's?"

She nodded. "You think I'll be able to come back home tomorrow?"

"The forensics guys will be finished tonight. I'll come by later and have a bit of a tidy up. The kids will never know what happened."

"Perfect." She kissed him on the cheek. "Let's go."

They drove for a while in silence. Mary normally asked for some terrible disco music while they drove, but today she just stared out of the window.

"I thought watching Guthrie fall would be the worst thing to happen to me this week," she said after a while.

"I'm sorry," Walker replied.

"You don't need to be sorry. It wasn't your fault."

"I guess not. I still feel sort of responsible though."

He could feel her eyes rest on his face.

"That's the whole point, Walker. I was responsible. I was conducting my own investigation, nothing to do with you being part of the police force. It's my job that caused this, not yours."

He felt it was best not to reply to this one. Instead, he changed the subject. "The guys are going to look into the Ginny Finlayson car crash. If there's anything we should know about it, they'll find it out."

"And you'll bring Finlayson in?"

"If we get enough evidence to do so. But we've probably already got enough to charge Cameron with the murder. DI Macleod will take some convincing to change his mind on that one."

"Then you've got to convince him. We can't let a murderer go free just because the suspect in custody is more convenient."

"I know," Walker said. They pulled into the drive at Mary's mum's house.

"Are you going to tell your mum what happened?" He asked.

"I'll have to. She'll know something's up. But I'll wait until the kids have gone to bed."

Walker reached over and held her hand. "I'm so glad you're okay."

Mary smiled. "Me too. You know, it's almost funny. Before

Cameron came I was waiting to talk to you about something. And I thought it was going to be a hard conversation, but then... Well, things changed. And it made me appreciate what we have right at this moment."

Walker wasn't sure he understood all that, but he was happy enough that Mary was reaching over to kiss him. She was safe and unharmed, and apart from that, nothing else mattered.

Chapter 31: Bernie

Bernie was feeling rather put out. She had called Mary after a garbled message about some sort of assault situation with Paul Cameron. Mary had explained everything.

"He came to your house? But you're saying you're okay?" Bernie asked. She wished that she could see Mary to check her out. Delayed shock was a killer.

"I'm fine. Really. It gave me a fright more than anything else. And he's going to be locked up for a long time now."

"But not for killing Alexander Guthrie."

"No," Mary agreed. "Walker isn't so sure, but I don't think he killed Guthrie. He was being blackmailed, but it wasn't Cameron that committed the murder."

Bernie stretched out her back. Not enough exercise and too much time researching on the laptop today. "You can tell Walker that I know from the horse's mouth that it was Annabel Guthrie who was doing the blackmailing."

"Are you sure you're happy to share that information?"

"Things change when someone attacks a member of my team. We need to put an end to this as soon as we can."

"So we're going to leave it to the police?"

"Are we hell. But I'm happy to have them along for a bit of

backup. Tell them to keep looking into Finlayson. If we can find a reason that Mrs Guthrie could use for blackmail then we might just be on to something."

"But they were friends, weren't they?" Mary asked. "Guthrie and Finlayson?"

"Yes, but –" Bernie looked at her phone's screen. "Hang on, I've got another call coming through. I'll speak to you later."

Bernie clicked off the call. She was impressed that Mary seemed to be holding it together. Maybe she wasn't quite as sappy as Bernie thought she was.

The other caller came up on her screen.

"You didn't hear this from me," Alice whispered. "But your old friend is on the move."

It took Bernie a second to get up to speed. "You mean Annabel Guthrie?"

"Yep. She snuck out of the house an hour ago while the police liaison was out having a ciggie. As you can imagine they're in the bad books."

"And it wasn't even a gas leak," Bernie tutted.

"What?"

"Nothing. The police have no idea where she's gone?"

"Nope. She's got her phone switched off, so even if we could check her location there's no help there."

"Okay, I'm on it."

"If you find her let me know, will you?"

"Of course," Bernie lied. She put her phone into her pocket and grabbed the car keys.

Once she was in the car she put her phone on speaker so that she could make another call.

"Hi Liz, it's me."

"I'm a... a little busy at the moment," Liz said, letting out little gasps of air.

"Just think 'soft cervix' as often as you can."

"Not helping. What did you want?"

"Annabel Guthrie is in the bloody wind. I need to know where she's gone."

"I don't... how can I find that out?"

"Aren't you the tech guru?"

There were some murmurs in the background that sounded like Liz's husband Dave. For some reason he didn't sound very happy.

"There might be one thing. Aah, let me get some gas and air." Liz disappeared for a few seconds, then came back. "Okay. When we realised how much Mrs Guthrie liked money, I checked out her social media. She loves putting pictures up: holidays, meals out, that sort of thing. She's put up plenty of photos of local places around Invergryff. Maybe there's something on that."

"Okay, send me the link."

"Will do. And Bernie?"

"Yes?"

"Feel free not to contact me for a bit."

Bernie clicked off the call and started driving. While she waited for Liz to send her the link to Annabel Guthrie's social media pages, she drove to the centre of town and parked near the Abbey. She knew it was unlikely the woman would go there, but Bernie wanted to see it again, to remember how this had all started.

Her phone pinged with a link. She clicked on the photo sharing site and started to scan through the pictures. It was just like Liz had said. Annabel was trying her best to present a perfect life. Every post was artfully shot, whether it was her lounging by the pool on holiday (wish you were here, besties!) or a bog standard cappuccino in a local coffee shop (#caffeine #blessed). It was enough to make Bernie want to puke.

Blackmail and overspending. A heady mix. Time to call in the reinforcements.

"I need some help," Bernie said as soon as Mary picked up the phone.

"Sure, what can I do?"

"I need to know something. If you were going to meet a blackmail victim in a coffee shop, would you choose the Ricciardo's on Blackwell Street or Mama J's on Cotton Street?"

"Ricciardo's," Mary said without hesitation. "It's big and busy. If I'm going to blackmail someone I want somewhere with lots of people so they won't come at me. Ricciardo's is the biggest in Invergryff, even though their pistachio eclairs are average at best."

"Thanks," Bernie said, hanging up the phone before Mary could say anything else. Time was ticking. Ricciardo's was close enough to walk if she moved quickly, and Bernie hadn't gone jogging four times a week for the last six years for nothing.

She set off at a steady pace, only wishing that she was wearing her proper running shoes. Luckily it wasn't quite time for the workers to come out of the nearby offices so the streets were clear. A few minutes later she arrived at the café.

It was part of a slightly run-down eighties brick building that had flats above it. Next door was a chemist and the bins outside could have done with being emptied. It wasn't the sort of place that Bernie usually went to – beige, carb-based food – but she was just about to go inside when she noticed that Annabel Guthrie's car was parked in the lane just to the right-hand side of the building.

Bernie felt a flush of triumph. She had found the woman before the police had. It was going to feel pretty damn good walking into the café and seeing the smug face disappear as she made a citizen's arrest.

She was about to go into the café when something nagging at her brain made her pause. Had there been a shadow in the driver's seat when she had glanced at the car? With a slight unease creeping up the back of her neck, Bernie walked up the lane.

She had only taken a few steps before she started to run. There was definitely something in the car and it wasn't moving. She was there in a matter of seconds. There was a body in the driver's seat and Bernie could tell from one glance that it was Annabel Guthrie.

Bernie yanked at the car door and it opened. The woman's head was turned away from her, but there was no movement, no sign of breathing. If only she had come a little sooner, been a little quicker on the uptake.

She touched her fingers to Annabel Guthrie's neck to check for a pulse even though it was probably too late. To her surprise, there was the faintest of rhythms. In a second, Bernie had her phone in her hand and was dialling 999.

"Wake up Annabel," she whispered as she was connected to the call centre that would send out the ambulance. "I'm not going to let you die before I send you to prison."

Chapter 32: Liz

Things were getting very hazy for Liz. Checks on the baby seemed to be going fine, although it was – according to the midwife – in no hurry to come and meet them. Liz thought this was rather selfish of the baby, especially when she was putting all the work in. The drugs were helping though, and the contractions were slightly less painful now.

"Um, you know how I said I wasn't going to let you see any more messages from the WWC?" Dave said from his position in the chair next to her bed.

"Yeah?"

"Walker has just sent me a message."

"You? I didn't even know he had your number."

"We meet up sometimes."

"Do you?" This was news to Liz. "When?"

"All right, we play online together. You know, classic first-person shooter games. That sort of thing."

"Is that what you're doing in your study when you say you're doing paperwork for the shop?"

"No comment. Anyway, he says that there was an incident at Mary's house. Apparently some guy called Paul Cameron turned up there, but he's been arrested and Mary is fine. He also said not to worry."

Liz bolted upright. "Mary's fine? But Paul Cameron was in her house? Give me my phone right now."

Dave sighed and handed it over. "I thought you might say that. Just try not to get too agitated. The midwife said she wanted to keep an eye on your blood pressure."

Blood pressure was the last thing on Liz's mind as she called Mary.

"Hello? Is the baby here?"

"Never mind the bloody baby, are you okay?" Liz said, twisting in the bed to get into a more comfortable position. "Dave said something about Paul Cameron being at your house."

"He just turned up," Mary said, and Liz could tell from her voice that she was shaken up. "I thought he might go for me, he was threatening me but… It all worked out okay. Mr Hoppy came to the rescue."

"Is that a weird pet name for Walker?" Liz asked.

"What? No. I hit him with a toy. And Walker did come in, only by that point I was fine. They've taken Cameron off to the police station."

"And you're sure you're okay?" Liz could feel another contraction building and it was hard to keep hold of the phone.

"Yes. Maybe. I think I'm all right. Look, Cameron was convinced that he was being set up for the murder. Bernie told me that Mrs Guthrie was blackmailing a whole bunch of people. Maybe one of them killed Guthrie instead. I've asked Walker to look into Sam Finlayson. He's the only other one with the opportunity to kill Guthrie."

"But no motive."

"Not as far as we know."

"I better go or there will be another murder," Liz said, looking at Dave's face. He gave her a nod when she hung up the phone.

The morphine must have kicked in because at that moment Liz checked her phone and saw a message from Bernie.

Might need an alibi later. Decided Mrs Guthrie no longer a suspect. Hope baby is here! B.

"Dave, will you tell them to give me a bit less drugs," Liz said, her head falling back on the pillow. "I just thought I read a completely nuts message from Bernie."

Her husband squeezed her hand as she took a puff of the gas and air. "Let's just forget about Bernie and the rest of them for a bit, okay?"

She looked into his eyes. "That sounds like a very good idea."

Chapter 33: Mary

It was getting late, but Mary was too wired to turn in for the night. She had hugged the kids extra tightly before helping her mum to put them to bed. It was hard not to think that she might not have had the chance if Paul Cameron had got his way.

She had given Nel an edited version of why she couldn't stay at home that night, but even with the worst of the details omitted, her mother had been horrified. Mary noticed that Nel kept looking out of the window as if they were still in danger.

"He's been arrested, mum," Mary said when Nel flicked the curtain aside for the third time. "They'll take him straight to prison until the court case."

"Weren't you frightened?" Nel asked her.

"Of course I was. And bloody angry. The cheek of the man!" Mary flushed at the memory of Cameron threatening her kids. It was lucky for him that he was behind bars.

"It's like you're a different person," Nel said.

Mary was just about to ask her mother if that was a compliment or an insult when her phone rang. It was Walker, which surprised Mary as she had only just managed to get rid of him. He had insisted on staying at Nel's until the kids had gone to bed. The fact that he was so attentive was rather sweet, but it was hard to get over the horrors of the afternoon when he kept asking if she was okay every five minutes.

"Sorry to bother you," he said when she picked up, "but I think I might need your help. Do you think you would be up for coming and meeting me?"

"I thought you told me to stay at my mum's place," Mary replied. "On the sofa. You even put on the Doctor Who box set on for me. We've not even got past the Ninth Doctor yet."

"I know. And believe me, I'd rather I didn't have to call you. But the thing is... Well, there's no easy way to say this, but Bernie's been arrested."

Mary was off the sofa and pulling on her trainers before Walker got to the end of the sentence.

"What the hell were you thinking?" Mary told him. "Bernie was only trying to help solve the case. I know she can be a nightmare but you didn't have to arrest her."

"It wasn't me," Walker said with a hurt tone. "And it wasn't anything to do with the case. At least, not directly. Listen, you can't tell anyone else about this just now, but she's been arrested because Bernie was found with Annabel Guthrie's body."

Mary gasped. "Sorry, what did you just say? Annabel Guthrie is dead?"

"No. I mean, not yet. Uh, that didn't sound right. What I mean is, hopefully she'll pull through. But she's been taken to hospital with head injuries. They think she might even slip into a coma."

"What does that have to do with Bernie?"

"As I said, she was found next to the body. And she's spent the last few days telling everyone how much she hates the woman."

Mary pinched the bridge of her nose. "Walker, you must know that Bernie would never kill anyone." Her general predilection for honesty kicked in. "At least, not without a damn good reason. And hating Mrs Guthrie wouldn't have been a reason to kill her. Let's face it, Bernie hates plenty of people and she doesn't go around murdering them all."

"I'm not sure that argument is going to work in her favour," Walker explained. "Look, it wasn't me that made the arrest. The Constables that found them did that. I'm going to do my best to speak up for her, but I think she could do with a friend at the station. Are you up to coming over?"

"Just try and stop me," Mary said firmly. She hung up the phone and got into her car. On the way to the police station she was careful to adhere to the speed limits, even though her heart was pounding. The WWC couldn't afford to lose another member.

Nel didn't seem too pleased when Mary rushed out the door, but she didn't say anything about it so it could have been worse. Mary had the feeling that she was in for a row with her mother in the near future, but that wasn't important right now.

She drove to the centre of town and parked across the road from the station. Mary was coming to know the police station in Invergryff quite well. She had picked Walker up after work a few times, and had even had the dubious distinction of being interviewed there herself several times.

When she got to Reception she saw Constable Harrow at the front desk.

"Are you here to give your statement about Paul Cameron?" the man asked. "I thought Walker was going to get you to write one at home?"

"He was. Is. No, I'm here for Bernie."

The man's expression was suddenly a lot less friendly. "You're with that woman, are you?"

"Yes. We work together. But I have to tell you that you had no business arresting her. Bernie would never be caught for murder."

"You mean she would never murder anyone?"

"Well, that's not quite what I said. But she would never be caught simply standing next to the body. I demand that you let me see her immediately! Um, please," she added, her vow to channel her inner Bernie failing at the first hurdle.

The Constable sniffed. "Mrs Paterson has not been arrested. Once we cleared up the little confusion that you mentioned, she was free to go."

"Oh. Then why is she still here?"

The man's eyes narrowed. "You tell me? As far as I can tell from the shouting, she's currently berating the Superintendent for his crime statistics."

"Ah. Maybe I should just go in and get her?"

"Please do. For all our sakes."

With that, the man on the desk buzzed her through to the main office. A female police officer led her through to the main office, where a small angry woman was standing with her arms folded in front of a group of weary-looking men in uniform.

"Bernie! Are you okay?"

"I'm fine. How are you? The Superintendent here was just explaining how a violent criminal was released from custody just in time to take you hostage."

"Oh, I'm not sure that's quite what happened," Mary said, feeling the need to stick up for the Superintendent purely because the man looked so miserable.

"Really? Seems that way to me. Paul Cameron was a suspect in a murder investigation, one with a history of aggravated assault and a clear vendetta against one of my most valued staff members."

"Most valued?" Mary grinned.

"Well, there are only four of us," Bernie added, which took a little of the shine off. "And on that note, I really can't afford to lose my friends to police incompetence. Or my enemies for that matter. Do we have any news on the condition of Annabel Guthrie?"

"None that I can tell you about," the Superintendent said. Mary felt sorry for the man. From what Walker told her, people at his level generally didn't have to deal with the general public and certainly not the ones as full of rage as Bernie.

"What about Finlayson? As Paul Cameron is in custody, he must be the prime suspect for the attack on Mrs Guthrie."

"We are in the process of locating Sam Finlayson," the Superintendent said.

"Aha! That means you've lost him too. Are you always this careless with your suspects?"

Walker poked his head around the door. "Would you like me to take Mrs Paterson and Mrs Plunkett home, sir?"

The Superintendent's shoulders relaxed. "Please do Sergeant. Walker here will help you with any further questions you might have."

"Is that a promise?" Bernie said as Mary took her arm and began dragging her from the room.

"Don't push your luck, Bernie," she whispered to her friend.

Bernie didn't even acknowledge that she had spoken. Walker gave Mary's arm a squeeze and managed not to speak to Bernie which showed that he was being remarkably restrained.

"There's a late-night cafe over there that does a good all-day breakfast," Mary said as they emerged from the police station. "If I go back to my mum's place now I'll only be in for an interrogation."

"All right," Bernie said, rubbing her eyes. "Let's see if they'll do me a smoothie. Do you know the only thing they offered me in that place was chocolate digestives. No wonder the police force is in ruins."

"They offered you biscuits?" Walker said, giving Mary a look. "They don't normally do that for anyone."

"Well, they did for me," Bernie said.

They were soon sitting together in the nearly empty restaurant while Bernie updated them on her discovery of Mrs Guthrie.

"Are we sure that Cameron couldn't have done it?" Walker said. "I mean, isn't there a chance that he could have attacked Mrs Guthrie and then gone around to Mary's place after?"

Bernie shook her head. "The timings don't fit. Annabel Guthrie didn't leave her house until after Cameron arrived at Mary's."

"But he could still be Guthrie's killer," Walker said stubbornly. "I mean, he attacked Mary. He has form for violence. So why don't you think it was him?"

"Because it was planned, just like Bernie explained. And does Cammie strike you as much of a planner?" Mary thought back to the man who invaded her home. The home of a copper's girlfriend. Not really the brightest move when you thought about it.

"Maybe not," Walker agreed.

"Then it's settled. Paul Cameron is not our murderer. Which

means the only other likely suspect is Finlayson."

"I just can't see it." Walker shook his head. "They were friends. Finlayson was genuinely upset that the man was dead. Why would he do it?"

"What if Finlayson was being blackmailed."

Walker leaned back in his chair. "We've looked into that. There's no suggestion of any communication between Mrs Guthrie and Finlayson."

"She's clever. She would have hidden it somehow."

"And you think Finlayson bashed her over the head too?" Walker grabbed her hand. "Look, if we're going to let Cammie off the hook for this murder, you better give me a damn good reason to start looking at someone else."

"It all comes back to the blackmail," Mary said and Bernie nodded in agreement.

"All right. We know she was blackmailing Cammie about his past. What the hell has Finlayson got to be blackmailed over?"

Mary clapped her hands together. "Now that's the perfect question."

Walker took a bite of his bacon roll and chewed it, his brow furrowed in thought. "Neil got back to me about the car crash. There was no post-mortem. No other cars involved and the driver dead, it wasn't felt that it was in the public interest to take the investigation any further."

"Very convenient."

Mary leaned back in her chair. "Does anyone else feel like we're nearly there on this one? Something is wrong with this car crash involving Finlayson's wife. Guthrie was interested in people confessing their sins, according to Mrs Button from the gift shop. Maybe he thought that Finlayson had something to confess?"

"Then why not tell the police?" Walker asked.

"Because he told his wife," Bernie said, a glint of excitement in her eyes. "And she saw a way to make money out of it."

"It's not quite enough to charge him," Walker said, "but certainly enough for an arrest. Only problem is he's not at home and no one has any idea where he is."

Bernie took a last swallow of her smoothie and stood up. "You're right. We better get going if we're going to catch Finlayson before he does something else stupid."

"Don't tell me you already know where he is?" Walker groaned.

"Not quite," Bernie said. "But I think I might have a map."

Chapter 34: Walker

Invergryff. A small town with some big problems, Walker thought. Was every place the same? Secrets lurking behind every door? He shook his head. That was the sort of dramatic thinking that he would criticise the WWC for. It was the job, no more or less. No need to get all romantic about it.

"Why do you have protein bars in your glove box?" Bernie Paterson asked. "They're full of refined sugar, you know. You should really make your own."

Walker looked in the rear-view mirror and raised an eyebrow at Mary sitting in the back. Why had he ever agreed to let Bernie ride in the passenger seat? Oh yes, because it was easier to just agree with anything she said. No wonder she was a good investigator.

"Why don't you tell me why I'm driving out of town when everyone else is looking for Finlayson in Invergryff?" Walker asked.

Bernie settled back in her chair. "It all comes back to Alexander Guthrie's job. He was a stonemason, and the thing about stonemasons is that they work at height. Just like my Finn does. Finn always says you wouldn't believe what you see when you're working on the roofs. The number of people that keep their curtains open... Well, like my nana used to say, they'd be better off saying their prayers."

Walker was getting one of what he thought of as his 'Bernie

headaches'. "Could you get to the point, please?"

"When I spoke to the cleaner, she said that Guthrie had been checking out a map of the Braes. I couldn't work out why he would have been looking at those areas. And being so furtive about it. But then I remembered that Ginny Finlayson's car crash had happened somewhere around here. Sure enough, when I checked out the names of the roads, the area that Guthrie was checking out on the map was the same place that Mrs Finlayson crashed her car."

"Why would he do that?" Mary asked, leaning forward into the space between the two front seats.

"I wasn't sure. But then I asked around to find out where he was working at the time. Do you remember that he had that eye injury? Liz's Dave was the one that checked him out. Luckily, to get his sick pay Guthrie had to fill in the insurance forms. I got Liz to find out what they said and they told us exactly where he was working."

"How did she manage that?"

"She has some friends in that world. Don't ask any more questions that you won't like the answer to."

Walker rolled his eyes but didn't make any more objections.

"On the night that Ginny Finlayson had her crash, Alexander Guthrie was working on an old railway bridge next to the canal. And if you look at the maps on your phone, it's on the road between the crash site and the Finlaysons' house."

Walker was beginning to follow her thinking. "He saw

something?"

"Or someone. I think on that morning he saw someone he recognised. The bridge is tall, so maybe he wasn't completely sure that it was his old boss, not at the time. It was only later on that he worked out the dates matched. And maybe when the Reverend started to talk about confession, it suggested something to the man. He started to wonder why Guthrie had lied about where he was the night his wife crashed the car. And unlike Annabel, I think Guthrie was a moral person. Unfortunately for him, he told his wife all about it."

"You might just have got it," Walker said, although his copper's brain was already trying to work out how they were going to prove any of it. "Finlayson said that it was just his wife in the car that night. But what if they were both in the car when it crashed? And Guthrie saw him walking home afterwards, leaving his wife behind him."

They had left the town by now and were climbing the hill into the areas known to locals as simply the Braes. Due to the altitude there weren't many trees around and the whole area was wild and windswept.

"What's the exact location of the crash?" Mary asked.

"I've put it into the Satnav," Walker said. "We should get there in a few minutes."

In typical Invergryff summer fashion, heavy rain had come in from the West and had started to lash at the windscreen.

"What do we do when we get there?"

"We're going to drive past first and see if we can spot him. Then I'll park up somewhere and we'll make our way back."

Sure enough, when they got to the bend in the road where Mrs Guthrie had been killed, there was a battered white van in a layby just over the road. Walker drove past a few metres until he was out of sight, then pulled the car over onto the verge.

"Can I bring my brolly?" Mary asked when they got out of the car.

"The 'I love Barbie' one?" Walker glared at her. "It's fluorescent pink! I want to approach Guthrie without him seeing us."

"Maybe not, then," Mary grumbled, pulling her hood tight around her hair.

Bernie at least looked like she was ready for anything. Walker's main worry was stopping her from running into the fray ahead of him. She didn't have any middle gears.

Walker took out his radio and called in to the station. He was put through to DI Macleod straight away.

"I hear you've found Finlayson."

"Yes sir. And I think there's a good chance he's Guthrie's killer."

"I'll send a backup car to your position. Are you happy to wait for them?"

Walker watched as Bernie was already striding towards the van.

"I think I might approach him myself first, sir. He might get spooked by a crowd."

"All right. But any sign of trouble and you're out of there."

"Sure."

Walker caught up with the two women.

"I need you to stay behind me," he explained. "If you're right about this, then he's killed, or attempted to kill at least two people."

Even Bernie couldn't argue with the logic on that one. She and Mary agreed to walk a few paces behind him as they came around the bend in the road where Mrs Finlayson had died.

Walker was beginning to rethink his strategy. He had no idea what sort of mood Sam Finlayson was in, but the fact that he had come up to the site of his wife's grave suggested he might be considering giving himself in rather than running. Instead of sneaking up on him, Walker decided it was best not to startle him.

"Let's walk directly up to the van," he explained to his companions. "You two stay behind me but still in my field of vision. Hopefully if he sees a couple of women with me he won't think I'm a threat."

As expected, there was a chorus of objections to that statement, but Walker ignored them. He started to walk forwards. They arrived at the van as the rain lessened to a steady drizzle.

"I'm going to move around to the front and give him a wave so he can see me. There's no sign he's a threat as of yet, but let's still be cautious."

He walked up to within ten feet of the van. He could just about make out Finlayson in the driver's seat staring out into the rain. Walker waved his arm and Finlayson raised his own hand in recognition.

"Right, I'm heading for the van. Stay behind me, and if anything happens, run back to the car. Backup is on the way."

Making no sudden movements, Walker walked around to the side of the van. Taking a deep breath, he reached for the door handle and pulled it open. Before Finlayson could object, Walker swung himself up into the passenger seat. It was only then that Walker noticed the sawn-off shotgun lying on the man's lap.

"Mary and Bernie, can you go back a bit please," Walker said, keeping his voice even. The passenger door was still open so that they could hear everything he said.

Bernie opened her mouth to challenge him, but Mary grabbed her arm.

"This is one of those times that we listen," she said, clocking the expression on his face. They took a few steps away. Walker would have preferred them away from the scene altogether, but he had a strong feeling that Finlayson hadn't brought the gun to shoot other people.

"Why don't you hand me that gun?" Walker asked.

Finlayson shook his head, but he didn't pick it up either.

"All right. Why don't we talk for a bit first?"

"If you found me here then you must know everything," Finlayson said. The man's face was pale and clammy, like he had eaten something that disagreed with him.

"I have some idea. But we'll need to hear it from you at some point."

"I'm not coming back to the police station," Finlayson said and Walker didn't like the waver in his voice. This was a man on the edge.

"Then why don't you talk to me here?"

"I could… I could stop you." Finlayson said. His hand flicked towards the shotgun.

"Mr Finlayson, just this week I have been punched on the chin by a man covered in superglue. I would really like to end this day without any more violence."

He stopped reaching for the gun and put his head in his hands. "I… Oh god, it's all such a mess. And AJ's wife as well."

"It looks like Mrs Guthrie is going to pull through," Walker said, watching as the man sagged with relief.

"I didn't want to kill her. Well, I did want to but… I just wanted it all to stop. I thought it was AJ that had been blackmailing me. I couldn't believe that he would be so two-faced. I mean, he even lent me money, and then he sent those emails. It was like he was laughing in my face. And then after he died I got another letter. I couldn't believe it! This time they were asking for even more cash. And when I worked out it was that woman…"

"The blackmail, it was all to do with the car crash, wasn't it?" Walker said, trying to make sense of the man's babbling.

Guthrie wiped his tears. "Yeah. I didn't realise anyone had seen me. After a year, I thought I'd got away with it."

"You were driving the car, weren't you?" Mary asked. She had crept closer now that the threat seemed to be less. Walker was still prepared to shield her if Finlayson went for the weapon.

The other man nodded. "I went to pick her up. I'd had a few beers, more than a few, but I didn't feel drunk. I guess I was driving a little too fast and I missed a bend in the road and I blacked out. When I woke up, the car was in the ditch and we had hit a tree. The windscreen was smashed and there were branches everywhere. I turned to look at Ginny and she was already gone."

"You made a bad decision," Bernie prompted.

"It felt like the only decision at the time. I felt terrible about it, but my wife was already dead. Nothing was going to bring her back. And I thought, well, why should my life be over too?"

"You put her into the driver's seat?" Walker could picture the scene.

"There was no one about. I managed to lift her out of the car and carry her around to the other side."

"And then you set up the scene to make it look like she had been drinking, didn't you?"

"There was a bottle of vodka in the car. I poured some of it away. Then I... I put some on her clothes so that she smelled of it. I tried to pour some of it into her mouth too."

Walker could see the disgust in the faces of the two women, but he made sure to keep his own expression neutral. He wanted to keep the man talking.

"I felt that for sure the police would work it out. I was terrified for weeks. Couldn't eat, couldn't sleep. I was signed off work with the stress. But no one said anything."

"Until the blackmail started."

"It was an email. I thought it was one of those junk things at first. But then I realised that whoever was sending them knew all about the crash. I was in trouble."

"When did you work out it was Guthrie?"

"I didn't! Not for ages. It came from one of these anonymous apps. I looked it up online and people use it because it's untraceable. Then AJ had his laptop open at lunch one day and I saw he had the same app installed."

"Not really proof, is it?"

"I wasn't completely sure until he started talking to me about confession. He said he'd heard a sermon from that Reverend guy, preaching about how there was no possibility of forgiveness without confession. And the way he looked at me,

I knew that he knew everything."

"So you pushed him off the scaffolding?"

"I didn't mean to! I went up there to talk to him." Finlayson's voice had changed into a desperate whine. "To tell him to stop asking for money. I told him he was being cruel, the way he had lent me money to help me out, while knowing the whole time the reason that I was so skint was that I was transferring him two grand every month."

"What happened then?"

"He denied it! I thought at the time he was still making fun of me, making out like I was too stupid to see through the lies. I didn't know until afterwards about Annabel."

Walker glanced at Bernie and Mary. "She was very clever," he said. "But why did you kill AJ?"

"It was... there was a scuffle. I grabbed him, told him to stop lying and he pushed me backwards. I grabbed a tool of some sort and hit him with it. I was so angry! And he started bleeding. He was so angry. He told me he was going to tell the police everything. He was leaning against the scaffolding and I sort of charged at him. Then he was on the ground."

Walker's eyes were still on the shotgun. "You managed to escape?"

"I knew the route out over the roof. Me and AJ chased some youngsters off there one time. We were, God, he was like a son to me. I felt terrible, but at least it was over."

"Until it wasn't," Bernie prompted

"That's right. I got another message. I couldn't believe it! But it didn't take me long to work out who must be sending them now that AJ was dead. And then I got a phone call from her this morning. One final payment and she'd never tell the police or anyone else what happened. Ten grand and she'd be out of my life forever. Only I didn't have ten grand. I went to meet her, to plead with the and somehow my hands were on her neck…"

"As I said, Annabel Guthrie is still alive. There's a chance that a judge will view your case with leniency, especially considering the blackmail. So why don't you let me take the gun."

Walker reached out in one steady movement and reached it out of Finlayson's lap, before the man had a chance to object. He placed it in the foot well at his feet and let his muscles unclench.

"It was my dad's, that gun. He was a farmer. I don't even know if it still works, but I wanted to… Well, to make sure I didn't spend the rest of my life in prison."

"If you kill yourself, Annabel Guthrie will get away with everything she's done. The least you can do is testify against her."

"Aye, that's something I can do," Finlayson said, wiping his eyes as the sound of sirens came down the road.

Chapter 35: Bernie

Mrs Guthrie looked so small and frail in the bed. Bernie could see the red lines on her eyelids that flickered as she slept. A weaker person might have felt sorry for her. But not Bernie Paterson.

"Are you sure we should wake her up?" Alice asked, looking nervous in her Specials uniform.

"The nurse said she was talking earlier. I wouldn't wake her up deliberately, but if someone was to bang this cupboard door over here," Bernie opened the door and slammed it shut. "Oh look, she's waking up."

Annabel Guthrie's eyes roamed the room, then widened when they spotted Bernie.

"Hello again," Bernie said with her biggest smile.

"What are you doing here?" Annabel said, her voice little more than a whisper. According to Walker, Finlayson had grabbed her by the neck, then slammed her head into the steering wheel. She was lucky to be alive. Less lucky that Bernie Paterson knew her way around visiting hours.

"I'm so glad you're feeling better. I've brought my niece here to explain some things to you."

"Your niece?"

The woman in uniform approached the bed. "I'm Alice and

I'm a Special Constable. I've been sent to explain the charges against you."

"Charges? But I was attacked!"

"Yes, and we're so glad that you are on the mend," Alice said with a bright smile.

"I can barely speak! Where are my nurses?"

"Someone brought in a lovely big box of chocolates for them," Bernie explained. "I think they'll be gone a while."

"You really are a pathetic little witch, aren't you?" Annabel said.

"Ah, insults, you really must be on the mend. But you should save your words for someone else. After all, I've come to tell you some good news. We've caught the man that killed your husband."

A flicker of confusion passed over the woman's face.

"You mean Sam Finlayson?"

"Yes."

"He's the one that attacked me."

"Correct. And have you any idea why he might have done that?"

The two women locked eyes for a few moments.

"None whatsoever," Annabel hissed.

Alice stepped forward, rustling some pieces of paper. "I don't think that's true, is it, Mrs Guthrie? Mr Finlayson told us that he attacked you because you were extorting money from him. And he added that the reason he killed your husband was that he thought that Alexander was the one sending him the threatening messages."

"You're going to believe the word of a killer?"

"Better than the word of a fraudster," Bernie snapped back. "Tell her what you found on her computer."

Alice nodded. "The thing is, it wasn't just the blackmail, was it? Bernie asked her friend Liz to take a look at your accounts as soon as we had access to your computer. We didn't know what we were looking for, but then I figured that blackmail wouldn't be a person's first attempt at obtaining money illegally. The sort of person who would do that would do all sorts of things. And sure enough we found them."

"Found what?"

"Years' worth of fraudulent dealings. We've only just started to look into them, but it looks like many stemmed from your time with the Social Work department. The perfect place, really, to provide you with access to the bank accounts of vulnerable people."

"You can't prove that."

"We will, given long enough. But for now, we've got the blackmail charge."

Annabel coughed, but neither of the other women offered her

a glass of water.

"I told you, Finlayson is lying."

"So you say," Bernie shrugged. "But while you were, you know, sleeping we checked out your phone."

"I wasn't sleeping. I was in a coma!"

"Still so dramatic!" Bernie shook her head.

"There's nothing on my phone anyway," Annabel said.

"Yeah, I bet you deleted everything. But it's funny, Sam Finlayson isn't quite as savvy as you are. He didn't delete anything. All the messages were just sitting there, right in his inbox for the police to find. And since that gave them your username, it wasn't hard to work out the rest."

Alice straightened her police vest. "We're working on the charges at the moment, but I suggest that you prepare your solicitor for a defence against multiple counts of fraud and misrepresentation, along with the extortion."

"And you just came to gloat about all this?" Annabel glared at Bernie.

"Partly, yes. But mainly I wanted you to see the person responsible for you spending a nice long stretch behind bars. I wanted you to consider whether if you hadn't been mean to me in school, you might have got away with it all. But then I realised that wasn't the case. Because this is my job, and I'm so good at it that I would have made sure you paid for your crimes whoever you were. Knowing it's you, with your mean little heart and your cruel little mind, it's just the icing on the cake."

Annabel Guthrie sat up, ready to reply, but Bernie was already walking out the door. She had work to do and the Wronged Women's Co-operative always needed her time. She wasn't about to waste a single second of it.

Chapter 36: Liz

The dark eyes stared at her, unblinking, through the transparent walls of the incubator.

"Hello little one," Liz whispered. She had just woken up from a nap to find a note from Dave saying that he had nipped out to phone his parents. Liz had already called her mum and Sean to let them know the news, then fallen into the sleep of exhaustion.

Not that she felt much less exhausted now, but those eyes gave her just enough energy to sit up and lift her child to her chest.

"Your name is Isioma. It means blessed, or lucky, and I think you are already. And your dad is white so he'll probably call you Issy, which will annoy your grandmother, but that's okay by me." She kissed the tiny forehead, just where it wrinkled above the nose.

A midwife came around with a cup of tea and Liz took it like it was the last drop of water in the oasis. "Thank you," she said.

"There are two women waiting to see you. Normally we just let the father in until visiting time, but if you're up to it I can let them in for a few minutes. One of them is annoying my nurses."

"Let them in," Liz said with a laugh.

"I haven't told you their names yet."

"You don't have to."

Bernie and Mary shuffled in, surrounding the bed with hugs and laughter.

"First turn for me," Bernie said, checking with Liz before scooping the baby out of her arms.

"Me next," Mary said. "I need something to cheer me up."

"What's wrong with Mary?" Liz asked.

Bernie grinned. "It seems that Mr Biggins and Mrs Mackenzie have found an amicable way of settling their dispute."

"My eyes!" Mary groaned. "I just went over to drop off their final invoices. I'll never look at a garden shed in the same way again. Not to mention the hosepipe."

"What, after all those rows they were… doing it?"

"Shagging in the shed," Bernie chuckled. "Who would have thought?"

"Uhh," Mary said, rubbing her eyes as if that would remove the images from her memory.

Liz burst out laughing. "Another success for the WWC, if a little different than what we normally get."

"And Annabel Guthrie is going to prison. Hashtag Blessed." Bernie quickly ran through her meeting with Guthrie. Liz didn't feel quite the same glee as her friend that the woman had been caught out, but she was glad that the Abbey case had concluded so successfully.

"She's just perfect, Liz," Mary said, staring into those dark brown eyes.

"I know," Liz replied. It might have had something to do with the drugs, but she was feeling very well-disposed towards her visitors. "Thanks for coming."

"Wouldn't have missed it for the world. Where's Dave?"

"He's off to call his parents, then pick up Sean. He can't wait to see his baby sister, even though he was hoping for a boy."

"Give us a shot will you Berns?" Mary asked and Bernie reluctantly handed the baby over.

Liz watched as Bernie sat on the edge of the bed, keeping an eye on the other woman.

"Are you crying Bernie?" Liz said, more than a little shocked.

"Just this hospital aircon," Bernie sniffed. "Plays havoc with my sinuses. Tip her head up a little, you're holding her too low."

Mary hid her grin, bending low over the sleeping baby and brushing her finger over her cheek. Liz felt a wave of utter contentment, whether from the diamorphine or the presence of her friends, she couldn't tell.

Epilogue

Mary watched as Sergeant Walker stood awkwardly next to Liz's bed. No matter how far equal rights have come, Mary thought, men still don't know what to do with themselves in the labour ward. He looked like he wanted to go outside and have a cigar and a game of rugby to get rid of all the oestrogen.

"Isn't she perfect?" Mary said, looking into the incubator where Liz's baby was fast asleep, so tiny and so precious.

"Adorable," Walker agreed. He had a box of chocolates in one hand and a congratulations balloon in the other.

Liz appeared out of the bathroom in a fluffy pink dressing room. "Thanks for waiting. I was dying to take a shower."

"When are you due home?"

"Sometime tomorrow. To tell the truth, I'm quite enjoying the rest. And the hospital food isn't too bad although they could use some hot sauce. When I go home I'm going to have to eat Bernie's lentil casseroles."

"A fate worse than death," Walker said.

"She means well," Liz said with a tired smile.

Mary knew not to overstay their welcome. "We'll just leave these here and let you get some sleep."

"Thanks," Liz said, already settling down in the bed.

The hospital had a garden at the front which was just a collection of benches before you got to the car park. Mary and Walker sat on a bench and watched as the men and women in hospital gowns pulled their IV drips out with them so that they could have a cigarette.

"Funny things, aren't they, human beings," Mary said tipping her head towards the patients huddled next to the doorway.

"You're not wrong," Walker replied.

"My mum said something the other day, and it's kind of been playing on my mind," Mary said as she watched him look around him, always with half an eye on the possible dangers. She had noticed that since Paul Cameron had invaded her home, Walker had kept just that little bit closer. It had been rather nice, which was only going to make the next few minutes worse.

"What was that?"

"She asked me if you wanted kids. In fact, she seemed surprised that we'd never had the conversation. And I realised that we'd never talked about it because I was scared of what you might say. Because I don't want any more kids. I'm done. And if you want a baby… if you need to have a child of your own, then you can't do that with me."

Walker looked kind of stunned. "All of that's been going around in your head for days?"

Mary nodded. "Yeah. I don't want to be the one that stops you from having a family of your own."

He looked down at his feet. When he spoke she knew he was choosing his words carefully. "The thing is, I sort of thought I was getting a family. With you."

A tiny crack opened up in Mary's carefully constructed armour. "What do you mean?"

"I know that they're not mine. Not yet, anyway. But I thought that maybe... Well, your kids have already got a dad, but I thought there might be room for a cool stepdad one day."

"You thought that?"

"Yeah. I mean, not at first. And not that time that Peter stole my radio and put it in the toilet cistern, but yes, I thought I might consider the position."

"And it wouldn't bother you? Not having your own biological kid."

"No. To tell you the truth, I'm a bit scared of babies. They're too fragile. I always think I'm going to drop them. And why don't they blink? Did you see little Isioma staring at me? She's like a snake."

Mary laughed. "Don't let Liz hear you say that. Are you being honest with me, though? You don't want a baby of your own?"

He pulled her into a hug.

"I think four children are quite enough for any man," he whispered, lips soft against her ear.

Mary kissed him full on the lips. "That is just what I wanted to hear."

Afterword

Thank you for reading another instalment from the – somewhat chaotic – world of the Wronged Women's Co-operative. Writing these characters has been an absolute blast from the moment they first inveigled their way into my brain. They don't seem to be showing any signs of disappearing soon and the sixth book in the series, *A Passion for Poison,* is available to order now.

Printed in Dunstable, United Kingdom